TOGETHER

by
NORMAN DOUGLAS

*"And he said unto me, Son of man,
can these bones live? And I answered,
O Lord God, thou knowest."*
Ezekiel xxxvii. 3.

to

ARCHIE and ROBIN

from their Father

NATAL PUBLISHING LLC
ARS LONGA, VITA BREVIS

Copyright[©] 2024 Natal Publishing

CONTENTS

Introduction (1)

The Brunnenmacher (11)

Tiefis (20)

Lutz Forest (28)

Blumenegg (37)

Father Bruhin (47)

Rain (56)

Ants (64)

Gamsboden (75)

Jordan Castle (87)

Rosenegg (96)

Valduna (104)

Old Anna (114)

Schlins (122)

INTRODUCTION

IT rains.

It has rained ever since our arrival in this green Alpine village; rained not heavily but with a grim Scotch persistence— the kind of drizzle that will tempt some old Aberdonian, sitting unconcernedly in soaking grass by the wayside, to look up and remark: "The roads is something saft." Are we going to have a month of *Landregen*, as they call it? No matter. Anything for fresh air; anything to escape from the pitiless blaze of the South, and from those stifling nights when your bedroom grows into a furnace, its walls exuding inwardly all the fiery beams they have sucked up during the endless hours of noon. Let it rain!

Little I thought ever to become a guest in this tavern, familiar as it is to me from olden days. They have made us extremely comfortable. Nothing is amiss, nothing lacking. Our rooms are large and well furnished. Certain preliminary operations were of course necessary in regard to the beds. Away first of all with the *Keilpolster*, that wedge-shaped horror; away next with the *Plumeau*, another invention of the devil. And breakfast always up here please, for both of us, in my room, at half-past seven; seeing that work begins at eight sharp. Not less than a litre of milk for my friend, and two eggs; he is a milk-and-egg maniac. I am past his stage, though still young enough to revel in that delicious raspberry jelly. Why is it almost unknown in England?

On one side of my room hangs an oleograph which depicts a gay sportsman aiming at some chamois from behind a tree at twenty-five yards' distance; such luck never came my way. The picture on the further side is still more suggestive—three roe-deer, hotly pursued by a dachshund; a pug-dog would have an equal chance of success. Cheerful pictures of this kind should hang in every room. I shall look at them whenever I feel jaundiced. Our tavern by the way is famous for its dachshunds. They have a couple of thoroughbreds, with faces like orchids, who eat and sleep most of the day and whose descendants are rapidly stocking the neighborhood. Their numerous progeny drop in for a visit from the remotest villages, and are coldly received by the parents. Just now the gentleman is asleep and his spouse, not for the first time, indulging in an agitated flirtation with one of her own remote descendants who has not yet found a home for himself: a very bad example to the rest of us....

Through the silvery curtain of drizzle I glance eastwards and recognize the old, old view, the earliest that ever greeted my eyes; for our nursery windows, up yonder, looked also towards the rising sun, and once, not in the day but late at night, I was lifted out of bed and placed on the window-sill to behold a wondrous thing—the sky all a-glister with livid rays. This aurora borealis is my first memory of life and the apparition must have been recorded in the newspapers of the day, since it was the only "Nordlicht" ever seen, to my knowledge, in the country; the vexed question, therefore, of a man's earliest memory could be settled, so far as I am concerned, if one had the energy to hunt up the files. There, confronting me on its hillock, stands the church with red-topped steeple. During the war, the authorities carried off the four bells to be melted down; three new ones have since been purchased at Innsbruck. They chime pleasantly enough, but not quite the same as of yore. One would like to hear the old ones again, for memory's sake, after all these years. How gayly they used to tremble on the air at midday, while one roamed about the hills at the back of the house. And how one rushed down to be in time for luncheon, seated on a fir-branch; an excellent method of progression on steep, slippery meadows, provided there be no stones or wasps' nests on the track. One day, long ago, we three slid in this fashion and at a breathless speed down the never-ending slopes of the Furkla alp above Bludenz. Nothing happened till about half-way, when the eldest felt a jolt, a slight cavity in the ground, and called out to me to beware. It was too late; I was pitched in and out again. My sister who followed, carrying less weight, came to rest there. The cavity was a wasps' nest. Eight stings....

And the church is backed by a mountain called Hoher Frassen; even at this distance one can detect a belt of green stretching across its middle near the scattered houses of Ludescherberg; wonderful, what manure will do! Everybody goes up the Hoher Frassen (*vulgo* Pfannenknecht) on account of the view, which is remarkable considering its low elevation of not even two thousand meters, though personally, if one must climb places like this, I should prefer the Mondspitze or Hochgerach. You can ascend in early morning from Bludenz or anywhere else, catch a glimpse of the Rhine and Lake Constance and snow peaks innumerable—of half this small province of Vorarlberg, in fact—and be home again in time for a late luncheon. Near the top is the now inevitable hut for the convenience of fat tourists. Cows pasture about the summit among the Alpine roses and dwarf pines.[1] Here, at the right season, you may capture as many Apollo butterflies as you please. A little boy and girl, scrambling homeward one day from this summit, dislodged with infinite trouble a huge bowlder and, while somebody was not looking, sent it on a career of delirious leaps down the incline above Raggal village. Such was its momentum after a couple of hundred yards that it went clean through a hay-hut, empty but solid, tossing its wooden blocks into the air as if they were feathers. The destruction of some poor peasant's property was considered a great joke. We laughed over it for weeks and weeks.

On the other side of our valley one can discern, despite the rain, those peaks of the Rhætikon group. They have been powdered with freshly fallen snow almost down to the Kloster alp, where cows are grazing at this moment. The Kloster alp, on which I have passed many nights with no companion save a rifle, is forever memorable in my annals as being the spot where, at the age of six, I smoked my first cigar. We were on an excursion and somebody—the little Dr. Zimmermann, I daresay, the blithe veterinary surgeon—gave me, doubtless at my repeated and urgent solicitation, a long black Virginia, a so-called rat's tail, the strongest weed manufactured by the Austrian Government. Delighted with my luck, I puffed through an inch or so. Then, without any warning, death and darkness compassed me about. Death and darkness! The world was

---

[1] Called "Latschen" hereabouts, because they are "gelegt"—pressed earthwards by winter snows; or else by the old Rhætic name of "Zuondra" which we sometimes twist into "Sonderinen." They are more generally known as "Legföhren." These groves of *Pinus pumilio* deserve careful protection; they shield the meadows below from the devastating effects of cloudbursts in the upper regions, from stone-cataracts and—by welding all successive snowfalls into that first one which lies anchored among their twisted limbs—from avalanches.

turned inside out; so was I. Not for several weeks did I try tobacco again; this time only a cigarette and in a more appropriate locality; even that made me rather unhappy. Here, on the cliffs just above the Kloster alp, you used to be able to gather a bouquet of Edelweiss with your eyes shut, so to speak;

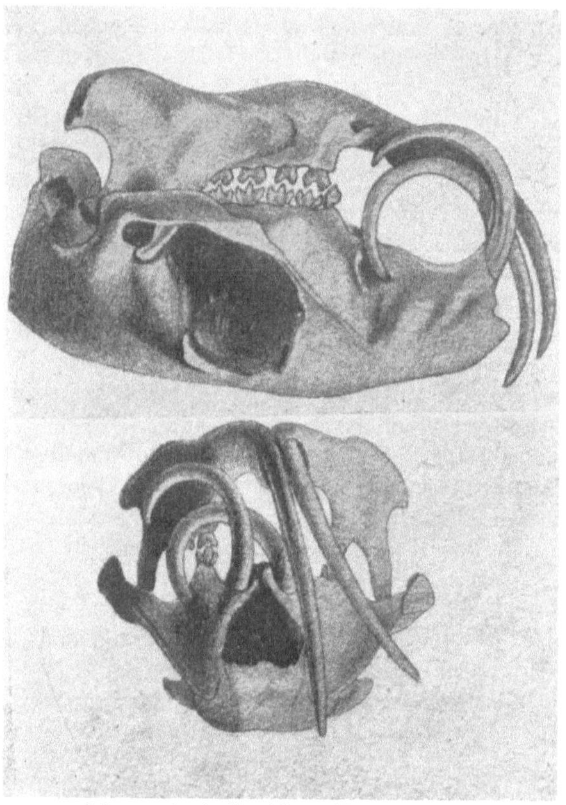

Marmot's skull with malformed teeth

here, among the tumbled fragments of rock further on, was a numerous colony of marmots. Never, in my bloodthirstiest days, had I the heart to shoot one of these frolicsome beasts, whose settlements are scattered over most of our mountains at the proper elevation. They call them "Burmentli" in our dialect—a pungent variety of alemannic—and their fat is supposed to cure every ill that flesh is heir to; it is chiefly on account of this fat that they have been persecuted in all parts of the Alps, and exterminated in not a few. Their cheery whistle carries half a mile; if you sit perfectly motionless, they will creep out of their burrows, one by one, and frisk and gambol around you. Once, at Christmas, a hunter brought me a hibernating marmot which he had taken, together with its whole family, out of winter-quarters. I put it, drowsy but half-awake, into a cold room, where it immediately rolled itself under a

bundle of hay. There it slept, week after week. A marmot in this condition is cold to the touch but not altogether stiff, and Professor Mangili calculated long ago that during the whole of its six months' lethargy it respires only 71,000 times (awake, 72,000 times in two days)—a veritable death-in-life! Mine displayed no resentment at being aroused now and then in a warm room; indeed, it behaved with exemplary meekness and allowed itself to be pinched or caressed or carried about; but preferred sleeping, and always seemed to say, in the words of the poet's sluggard, "You have waked me too soon! I must slumber again." When summer came round, we took it back to its old home, where it trotted off without a word of thanks, as if the past experiences in our valley had been nothing but a silly dream.

One would hardly think that marmots ever fed each other, yet a skull in my collection makes me wonder how this particular animal, an old beast, can have survived without receiving nourishment from its fellows. It was shot near St. Gallenkirch in the Montavon valley on September 12th, 1886; and is remarkable since, in consequence of what looks like the fracture of a single incisor tooth, the lower jaw has been partially and slowly displaced, shifted to one side of the upper—at the cost, no doubt, of incessant pain. What happened? All four incisors therewith became not only useless but an intolerable hindrance; lacking the necessary attrition, they grew ever longer in mammoth-like curves, and sharply pointed; the shortest—the injured one, which is still deprived of enamel at its extremity—measures six and a half centimeters in length, the longest all but eight; and one of them, in the course of its circular development, has actually begun to bore into the bone of the upper jaw. I am not much of a draftsman, but these two sketches will suffice to give some idea of the freak specimen. A squirrel with somewhat similar dentition was described in the "Zoologist" (Vol. IX, p. 220). Here was one marmot, at least, who must have been glad when summer food-problems were over, and it grew cold enough to scuttle downstairs again for a six months' rest. And some of them sleep in this fashion for eight months on end. What a sleep! Why wake up at all?

Food-problems of our own——

They are non-existent. This region has suffered *relatively* little from the effects of war; it is a self-supporting district of peasant-proprietors where nearly every family possesses its own house and orchard and fields and cattle; the ideal state of affairs. Nothing is lacking, save tobacco and coffee. To obtain the first, one plagues friends in England; instead of the second, we have to put up with cocoa, a costive and slimy abomination which I, at least, will not be able to endure much longer. Prolonged and confidential talks with the innkeeper's wife—his third one, a lively woman from the Tyrol, full of fun and capability—have already laid down the broad lines of our bill of fare. I must devour all the old local specialties, to begin with, over and over again; items such as *Tiroler Knödel* and *Saueres Nierle* and *Rahmschnitzel* (veal, the lovely Austrian veal, is scarce just now, but she means to get it) and brook-trout *blau gesotten* and *Hasenpfeffer* and fresh oxtongue with that delicious brown onion sauce, and *gebaitzter Rehschlegel* (venison is cheap; three halfpence a pound, at the present rate of exchange); and, first and foremost, *Kaiserfleisch*, a dish which alone would repay the trouble of a journey to this country from the other end of the world, were traveling fifty times more vexatious than it is. Then: cucumber salad of the only true—i. e., non-Anglo-Saxon—variety, sprinkled with *paprika*; no soup without the traditional chives; beetroot with cummin-seed, and beans with *Bohnenkraut* (whatever that may be); also things like *Kohlrabi* and *Kässpätzle*—malodorous but succulent; above all, those ordinary, those quite ordinary, *geröstete Kartoffeln* with onions, one of the few methods by which the potato, the grossly overrated potato, that marvel of insipidity, can be made palatable. How comes it that other nations are unable to produce *geröstete Kartoffeln*? Is it a question of

Schmalz? If so, the sooner they learn to make *Schmalz*, the better. *Pommes lyonnaises* are a miserable imitation, a caricature.

In the matter of sweets, we have arranged for *Schmarrn* with cranberry compote, and pancakes worthy of the name— that is, without a grain of flour in them, and *Apfelstrudel* and— quick! strawberries down from the hills, several pounds of the aromatic mountain ones, to form those wonderful open tarts which are brought in straight from the oven and eaten then and there, hot—if you know what is good. Should the weather grow sultry, I will also make a point of consuming a bowl of sour milk, just for the sake of auld lang syne. It may well ruin my stomach, which has acquired an alcoholic diathesis since those days.

There! A change of food, at last.

Whether Mr. R. will take to this diet is another matter. I should be in despair if he were a true Frenchman, for your Gaul, in this and other matters, is the most provincial creature in the world; like a peasant, he can eat nothing save what his grandmother has taught him to think eatable. Mr. R., luckily for him, is French only from political necessity. And besides, persons of his age should never be encouraged to express likes and dislikes in the matter of food; it is apt to make them capricious or even greedy, and what says the learned Dr. Isaac Watts, from whom I quoted a moment ago? "The appetite of taste is the first thing that gets the ascendant in our younger years, and a guard should be set upon it early." How true! Nobody is entitled to be captious until he has reached the canonical age. After that, he has acquired the right of being not only critical, but as gluttonous as ever he pleases.

Here, meanwhile, are the latest statistics of our village. It contains about seven hundred inhabitants, three hundred cows and calves (most of them on the mountains just now), five taverns, and three *Dorftrottels* or idiots, of the genuine Alpine breed. Mr. R. is dying to have a look at them as soon as the weather clears; and so am I. There is a fascination about real idiots. They have all the glamour of a monkey-house, with an additional note of human pathos.

A heated discussion after dinner with Mr. R.—one of our usual ones—as to the right meaning of the English words "still" and "yet" which, like "anybody" or "somebody," he refuses to distinguish from each other. On such occasions, he complains of the needless ambiguity and prolixity of my language; I retort by some civil remark about the deplorable poverty of his own. I should explain that I hold certificates as teacher of French and English, and am in possession of an infallible coaching method (a family secret) for backward or forward pupils; and that this is not the first time I have endeavored to instill a little knowledge of English into the head of Mr. R. who, for all his faults, is a companionable young fellow with certain brigand-strains in his ancestry that go well with those in mine (*vide* Peter Hinedo's "Genealogy of the most Ancient and most Noble Family of the Brigantes, or Douglas," London, 1754).

That astonishing French education.... What is one to do with people, future candidates for government posts, who cannot tell the difference between an adverb and a conjunction, who, if you ask them to define a reflexive verb, gaze at you with an air of injured innocence, almost as if you had asked them to say what is the capital of China, the position of their own colony of Obok, and whether Chili belongs to Germany or to Austria? They learn none of these things at school; or if they do, it is in some infant class where they are forgotten again, promptly and forever. Instead of this, they are crammed with microscopic details, under the name of "Littérature," concerning the lives of all French writers that ever breathed the air of Heaven, and with a bewildering mass of worthless physical formulæ, enough to daze the brain of a Gauss. What Mr. R. does not know about convex lenses and declination needles and such-like balderdash is not worth knowing; his acquaintance with every aspect of Molière's life and works is devastating in its completeness, and makes me feel positively uncomfortable. Now Molière was doubtless a fine fellow, but no youngster has any right to know so much about him. I only wish they had taught him a few elements of grammar instead.[2]

---

[2] He has surprised me, of late, by a new acquirement: a considerable familiarity with Polish history. They only began to teach it quite

It is too late now. He laughs at grammar—a frank, derisory laugh. In other words, my task is rendered none the easier by his serene self-confidence. He does not share my view that his English is still rudimentary, though he admits that it may require "a little polish here and there." Everything in the nature of a difficulty or exception to the rules is an *idiom*—not worth bothering about. He conjugates our few irregular verbs as if they were regular; go, go'ed, go'ed; find, finded, finded; and gets in a towering passion, not with me but with the language, whenever I have to set him right. Their mellow auxiliaries of "should" and "can" and all the rest of them, so useful, so reputable, so characteristic of the versatile genius of England, are treated as a perennial joke; indeed, it is a wretched idiosyncrasy of his to discover fun in the most abstruse and recondite material. (He nearly died of laughing the other day, because I told him that the Neanderthal race of man was less hairy than the *Pithecanthropus erectus* of Java; and failed to explain why such a bald scientific statement of fact should provoke even a smile.) Simple phrases like "Est-ce que l'enfant n'aurait pas dû acheter le chapeau?" give birth to English renderings that would send any less patient tutor into convulsions; renderings such as you might expect from the average Englishman when asked to put into French "If I had not noticed it, you would not have noticed it either (using *s'en apercevoir*)."

To all my suggestions that it might be well to study this or

---

recently, he says; and thereby hangs a tale. It would seem that an ukase has gone forth from educational headquarters in Paris, to the effect that the youth of the entire country is to be brought up in the belief that the Poles, the old friends of France, are a prodigy among nations; every phase of their contemptible politics and degrading parliamentary wrangles during the last few centuries has to be regarded as of epoch-making importance—as opposed to the futile history of their enemies on the East. Nothing, in short, is good enough for Poland; nothing bad enough for Russia. And all because a misguided pack of French capitalists, after those Toulon celebrations, lent their millions to Russia, expecting to receive the usual three hundred per cent profit which is not yet forthcoming and, let us hope, never will be. An interesting example by what means "patriotic" convictions are nurtured, and for what ends.

that more conscientiously, I receive the stereotyped reply "I know my *vocables*"; as if the possession of an English vocabulary were synonymous with the possession of English speech. It is perfectly true; he has a fair stock of words, and nobody would believe what can be done with our language until he hears it handled by a person who knows his *vocables* (and nothing else) after the manner of my pupil; I often tell him that he could make his fortune in England, on the music-hall stage, with that outfit alone. Nevertheless, strange to say, he was nearly always the first in his English class at school. Vainly one conjectures what may have been the attainments of the rest of them or, for that matter, of their teachers.

So he studies two hours a day with me and two hours alone, preparing for an examination in October; and that is his *raison d'être* in this country. He has just given me, to correct, a translation from a book full of "thèmes et versions," all of which are too difficult for him; this one is his English rendering of a stiff piece that describes P. L. Courier's disgust at the French Court. It is a noteworthy specimen of my pupil's command of *vocables* and of nothing else; a document which I should not hesitate to set down here, in full, could I persuade anybody into the belief that it was authentic. That is out of the question. People would say I had wasted a good week of my life, trying to manufacture something comical.

Instead of this "anglais au baccalauréat" we have lately begun a course of Grimm's Fairy Tales which are nearer to his level, and I am realizing once more what this stuff, so-called folk-lore, is worth. A desert! For downright intellectual nothingness, for misery of invention and tawdriness of thought, a round half dozen of these tales are not to be surpassed on earth. They mark the lowest ebb of literature; even the brothers Grimm, Germans though they were, must have suffered a spasm or two before allowing them to be printed. Fortunately Mr. R.'s versions of this drivel are far, far superior to the original; they beat it on its own ground of sheer inanity; and I am carefully collecting them to be made up, at some future period, into an attractive little volume for the linguistic amateur.

THE BRUNNENMACHER

NOW what may that old *Brunnenmacher* have looked like? I never saw him. I only know that, like my friend his son, he was the official water-expert of the town of Bludenz, that he was older than my father, and every bit as incurable a *Bergfex*—mountain-maniac. His nick-name, "Bühel-Toni," suffices to prove this. Those two were always doing impossible things up there at the risk of their lives (it was thus, indeed, that my father was killed) either together, or alone, secretly, in emulation of each other. For in those days the whole of this province was virgin soil, so far as climbing was concerned, and numberless are the peaks they are supposed to have scaled for the first time. Yet neither of them, it seems, had ever tackled the Zimba, the noblest of those pinnacles of the Rhætikon group which I can see from this window, out there, on the other side of the valley, covered with fresh snow wherever snow can come to lie among its crags. The Zimba rises to a height of 2640 meters and was regarded as inaccessible by local chamois hunters who, for the rest, were under no obligation to scramble up places of this kind, their game being abundant lower down. Inaccessible! That annoyed these two *Bergfexes* all the more.

"Are you never going to try?" my father would ask.

Said the Brunnenmacher:

"I am an old man, and have at least three times as many children dependent on me as you have. That makes a difference. Besides, you are rich. Rich people can afford to break their necks. Aren't you ashamed of yourself? There it is, staring you in the face all day long. I could never resist the temptation, if I were in your place. Only think: it would be quite an unusual kind of honor for you, an Englishman, to have been the first up there. In fact, I confess I should feel a little jealous and sore about it, myself."

So it went on for months or years, and each time they met, the Brunnenmacher would say:

"So-and-so now thinks of trying the Zimba. Are you going to let him have it his own way? Is he to get all the glory? Now's your chance," or else: "How about the Zimba? Still afraid? What a scandal. Ah, if I were only a few years younger!"

At last my father could bear it no longer and slunk out of

the house one afternoon on his usual pretext—when anything risky had to be done—of going after chamois. He rolled himself in his blanket at the Sarotla alp, near the foot of the peak, and next day, somehow or other, set foot on the virgin summit. Imagine his disgust on finding there a *Steinmandl*, a cairn, containing a bottle with an affectionate letter to himself from "Bühel-Toni" who had sneaked up ages ago, all by himself, without saying a word to any one.

That is the history of the Zimba, which is now climbed by numerous tourists every year. No wonder; since all the difficult places have been made easy. Even so, the mountain has claimed its victims—three, within the last few years; one of them a tough old gentleman who, to test his nerve and muscle, insisted on "doing" the Zimba once a year. It was a sporting notion; the Zimba did him, in the end; he lies buried in the new Protestant cemetery at Bludenz. And if you like to scramble up from the Rellsthal flank, you may still have some fun. Not long ago a tourist actually died of fright while climbing down here. He had gone up by the ordinary route to the satisfaction of his guide who, being from the Montavon valley and anxious to get home as soon as possible (this is my own assumption) took him down by this almost perpendicular "short cut." At a certain point the tourist declared that he could go neither forwards nor backwards, and was going to die then and there. Which he straightway proceeded to do, rather foolishly. But there are no limits to what a real tourist can accomplish. Along the extremely convenient track which scales the cliff between the Zalim alp and the Strassburger hut (Scesaplana district) two young men contrived to slip; they were shattered to fragments. Cleverest of all was the gentleman who lately achieved the distinction of dying from exposure on the Hoher Frassen. He ought to have left us word to say how the thing was done.

We do not always realize the difficulties of the pioneers. Among other matters, there were no shelter huts in those days. That which lies below the Zimba, on the Sarotla alp, is one of some fifty now scattered about the hills of this small province. The earliest of them all was the Lünersee hut which bears the name of my father; he was then president of our local section of the Alpine Club. Built for the convenience of visitors to the Scesaplana summit, this hut was swept into the lake long ago, with all it contained, by an avalanche. It is time another avalanche came along, for the place has grown into a caravanserai of the rowdiest description. Altogether, selfish as it may sound, I should not be sorry to see every one of these structures burnt to the ground, or otherwise obliterated. Their primary object, to afford shelter to *bona fide* climbers, is laudable; what they actually do, is to serve as hotels—not bad ones, either—to a crowd of summer visitors whose faces and clothes and manners are an outrage on the surroundings. Abolish the huts, or cut down their comforts and menus to what a climber might reasonably expect, and the objectionable "Hüttenwanzen" would evaporate. What are they doing among these mountains? Let them guzzle and perspire in Switzerland!...

My friend the younger Brunnenmacher, son of "Bühel-Toni," was also official water-specialist and *Bergfex*; he may well have been the image of his father since, from all I have heard, he had the same character and therefore, according to a theory of my own, must have resembled him also in person. If that be so, we may take it for granted that the father was an unusually hirsute creature. The mere sight of his son, at the Bludenz swimming baths, used to send us into fits. Nobody had ever seen such a "Waldmensch." He might have been a gorilla in this respect—an uncommon kind of gorilla; for not every gorilla, I fancy, can afford to wear a regular parting down its back. No gorilla, either, could climb in better style; or smile, if they smile at all, to better purpose. The Brunnenmacher's laughing face charmed away hunger and fatigue and wet clothes and all the ills of mountaineering. It may seem far-fetched to apply the terms "ingenuous" or "childlike" to the smile of a bearded monster of forty, but there are no other epithets available for that of the Brunnenmacher. It rose to his lips, on seeing you; it hovered there day and night, waiting for your appearance. Doubtless he had a peculiar affection for me, as being my father's son; everybody found him a lovable person.

His weather-proof good humor must have helped to establish his reputation as a guide; that, and his jovial blasphemies. They made you laugh, and a guide who makes you laugh has already gone a long way towards gaining your friendship. Once you persuaded the Brunnenmacher to begin some story of his, which was not difficult, you were sure to get an adequate amount of playful bad language thrown in. An infallible method of getting more than this adequate amount was to make him relate his experiences of a trip to America, and of the agonies of four days' sea-sickness on an empty stomach. This narrative bristled with swear words; it ended in a fixed formula: "Jo, Himmelherrgottsakraméntnochemol, do honni grod gmeint i müest ussm grosse Zähe uffi kotze!" which might as well be left untranslated ...

There is a curious cave near Bludenz called the *Bährenloch*, the bear's cavern; it lies at the foot of the cliffs above the road to Rungalin village—not the field path, but that which skirts the hills. I say curious, because it is plainly not a natural cave; it is an artificial one and has been hacked by human hands out of the limestone; when, by whom, and for what purpose, no one knows. The chisel-marks are quite plain, once you are well inside. It is roughly quadrangular in shape and about the height of a man at the entrance; half way through, it takes a slight bend to the right and, growing narrower and narrower till you can hardly turn round, ends abruptly, as though the builder had grown weary of his toil, or disappointed with its result. The work of a mediæval anchorite? I doubt it. Such a person would have contented himself with a domicile less than half its length. Perhaps some crazy enthusiast dug it long ago, in the hope of discovering gold or what not among the bowels of those cliffs.

The younger Brunnenmacher first took me there, and how he managed to hit upon the precise locality of this grotto remains a mystery to me. Not only was the steep woodland below much thicker in those days—almost impenetrable, in fact—and without any trace of an upward path, but the entire base of the cliffs was defended by so dense a mass of brushwood that we had to crawl through it on hands and knees. How did he contrive to ascend undeviatingly to the cavern's mouth? A few yards astray, and we should have been lost in that jungle where one could barely move, and had no means of seeing to right or left. All this sounds incredible at present. Most of the brushwood has been uprooted and the forest thinned out to such an extent that it has become quite transparent; moreover, that meritorious "beautification-society" of Bludenz constructed, among many other things, a convenient zigzag path which will lead you after fourteen windings to the very entrance of the *Bährenloch*. The horse-shoe bats, the greater and the lesser, which I used to capture here and take home as pets, may well have deserted the place; likewise the young foxes and badgers we unearthed in the neighborhood. One of these badgers grew so tame that he followed me about everywhere, and would even take me for rides on his back. I should like to see him do it nowadays.[3]

This Brunnenmacher seems to have made up his mind that I was to become a climber like himself. He took me in hand. He made me trot miles and miles, as it seemed, up the then almost trackless Galgen-tobel and showed me the *fons et origo* of the Bludenz water supply, as well as a spot where you could discover a certain vitriolic mineral by the simple process of applying your tongue to the rock; and still further afield, into the upper regions of the Krupsertobel, and down its savage bed. Then came the turn of the mountains—Scesaplana, to begin with. As guide, he had already gone up there some seventy times, and even I got to know it so well in later years that I could have walked up in blackest midnight. Next the Sulzfluh, famous as a haunt of the Lämmergeier; and so on. One of the last of

---

[3] We walked up to the *Bährenloch* last week. The path is neglected and quite overgrown in places; the cave seems to have lost its popularity since the war. I was glad to see that old yew tree—rather a rare growth hereabouts—still clinging to the rock near its entrance. We went in with candles and saw one bat fluttering about; I felt no great desire to take it home with me. The pets one kept! Guinea-pigs, first of all, *Meerschweinle* which, in a burst of infantile humor, I used to call *Immermehrschweinle*, alluding to their miraculous fecundity. Not a bad joke, now I think of it. And the last was a black squirrel, that ended in pitiable fashion. I took it out of its nest and brought it up on the bottle, like a baby. It grew to be my companion all the time, free to come and free to go, and there was nothing I could not do with it; we were really devoted to each other. Afterwards, having to leave the country, I gave it in charge of a certain female relative who also loved it. The cage was placed on the top of one of those enormous stoves of green majolica tiles. Winter came, and the maid lighted the fire, forgetful of the cage above. Then she remembered, and rushed back into the room. Too late! The poor beast had meanwhile been slowly, quite slowly, roasted to death. No more pets after that.

these trips was up the Säntis, the shapely peak across the Swiss frontier, which seems to close up our valley to the west. We came back with our pockets full of rock-crystals.

So I pursue the memories, as they rise from the past, of those old days of the Brunnenmacher. He died a good many years back. But he has left behind a sturdy brood of children— I know not how many; dozens of them, let us hope, to inherit his smile....

That Säntis mountain, which I have just mentioned, has a bad name at this moment. There was a foul murder done here, some months ago; the married couple in charge of the observatory near the summit were found killed at their post. Nobody could guess who the assassin was, nor what his object might have been, till the body of a young man was discovered in some hut not far away. He had committed suicide; and he was the murderer. So far as I could gather, this youngster was of decent birth but, owing to excesses of one kind or another, had lost all balance and self-respect. One thing, nevertheless, he preserved intact: an intense love of the Säntis, his native mountain, which he seems to have regarded as a sort of private domain. He knew its territory inch by inch and could never bring himself to forsake it; this affection, indeed, was his undoing, for after the crime he made no attempt to quit the country, as he easily might have done. The all-absorbing attachment to this piece of ground kept him chained there, and it was supposed, though nowise proved, I fancy, that he killed the old people out of an insane envy, and in the equally insane hope of being thereafter installed at the observatory as their successor, and having the Säntis all to himself for the rest of his life. Murders are committed for a considerable variety of amorous motives, but seldom for one of such a glacially nonsexual and idealistic tinge; it is the kind of etherealized horror that might be imagined to take place on some other planet. Altogether, an interesting problem in psychology, if the facts they gave me are correct. To fall in love with a mountain is not the common lot of man. And so disastrously!

It was a tragedy of unreciprocated passion, from beginning to end. The Säntis is no longer in the first flush of youth; it can be trusted, I feel sure, to behave with perfect decorum under the most trying and delicate circumstances. Its reputation, previous to this little affair, had been of the best; nor is there any reason to suppose that it gave its brain-sick admirer the slightest encouragement to act as he did, or to think himself singled out for favors denied to the rest of us. The locality is doubtless attractive, as such places go, but that is not its own fault—who ever heard of blame attaching to beauty?—so attractive, that a man might well be pardoned for growing fond of it, and fonder, and fonder. Even in the case of superlative fondness, I, at least, would still try not to feel jealous of other people's familiarity with its charms, and would certainly think twice before murdering a respectable married couple *pour ses beaux yeux*.

I have now seen four generations of these delightful folk who own our tavern, the latest arrival being a great-grandchild of the first. Though barely born, it already wears a laughable resemblance to its grandfather.

He is the present head of the family, a village magnate who knows the ins and outs of the countryside as well as any one alive; a Nimrod in his day, and the only marksman, beside my father, to whom they hung up a diploma of honor in the Ludesch shooting range; he has lived for years in Milan and traveled, officially, to Vienna, to set forth to the Government some claim of our district. The face might be that of one of those good-natured but intelligent Roman emperors like Titus, with round head and ruddy hair; a face such as you find all over the Roman province to this day, and all over this province as well. His family came originally from the Bregenzerwald region, at the back of our hills, and is connected with that of Angelika Kauffmann who was born there.[4]

Having been friends with him for the last half century, we

---

[4] Here is a local and contemporary appreciation of this glory of art. "Mit höchstem Rechte verdient hier die aus dieser Landschaft gebürtige Angelika Kaufmann eine Stelle. Dieses mit den seltensten Vorzügen des Genies ausgestattete Frauenzimmer macht wirklich in der Malerei Epoche, und lebt diesmal als eine der berühmtesten Künstlerinnen des sich neigenden achtzehnten Jahrhunderts, in glücklicher Ehe in Rom, zur Ehre ihres Vaterlandes, das auf sie stolz seyn darf." (Vorarlbergische Chronik. Bregenz, Brentano, 1793, p. 81.)

never lack subjects of conversation; there is fresh ground to explore as often as we meet, and old ground to traverse again. What I now want to know is this: how about the rain? Are we in for a *Landregen*? He thinks not; the weather is too cold, and snow lies too low; where his own cattle are, on the alp of Zürs near Lech, it must be lying at this moment. Unless the weather clears, he will have to go up and look after them; also on account of the foot-and-mouth disease, which has broken out in the neighborhood. Lech: who has the chamois shooting there? Nearly all the shoots in the country, he explains, have been taken by Swiss, and no wonder; look at their exchange! And what of the projected *Anschluss* (annexation) to Switzerland? Well, Germany would be better, on the whole. Besides, the truth of the matter is (laughing) the Swiss won't have us; they say we are too Catholic and too lazy and too fond of drinking. As if our people could afford to pay for wine nowadays! By the way, just try this *Schnapps*, as a curiosity.

It was juniper-spirit, of the year 1882. With all respect for its antiquity, I found myself unable to appreciate the stuff. Then he gave me, as an antidote, some of his own *Obstler* (made of apples) only three weeks old. A little crude, but of good promise. So we went through the lot. His own *Zwetschgenwasser*—excellent! Then Kirsch, from the neighboring village of Tiefis, which makes a specialty of this *Schnapps*, distilled from the small mountain cherries; of mighty pleasant flavor. Next, Enzian; the product of the yellow Alpine gentian. Whoever likes Enzian—and who can help liking it?—will have nothing to say against that of our Silberthal, which has a well-deserved reputation for this brand. *Beerler*, I enquire? No, he says; nobody makes bilberry-spirit any more.

"Which is a pity."

"This infernal war——"

"It has shattered all the refinements of life."

So we discuss the world, and presently the proprietress comes up to announce that she has discovered coffee. I thought she would! She sent to Bludenz for it, on the sly. Now what, I ask, is her particular method of roasting?

"Why, in the oven, of course; and very carefully. Then, when the beans begin to sweat, and are neither lighter nor darker than a capuchin's frock, I take them out and place them, steaming hot, into a glass jar and cover them at once with a thick layer of powdered sugar. There they get cold slowly and are obliged, you see, to draw in again all the fragrance which they would otherwise have lost. Isn't that your English way?"

I wish it were....

TIEFIS

AREALLY fine morning at last; glorious sunshine.

"Now for those idiots," says Mr. R., and so do I. We have found out about them, from the inn-people.

It appears that two, a man and a woman, come from the Walserthal, which has always been famous for its crop of imbeciles; the third was born at Raggal, likewise fertile mother of idiots, because everybody marries into his own family there. These Raggalers are such passionate agriculturalists and so busy, all the year round, with their fields and cattle, that they refuse to waste time scouring the province for so trivial an object as a wife with fresh blood, when you can get a colorable substitute at home. Our particular idiots live, all three of them, on the road to St. Anne church, in that workhouse which, so far as I know, has sheltered from time immemorial the poor of the district, the aged, the infirm of mind or body. There is always a fine assortment of wrecks on view here. Sisters of Charity look after them.

Sure enough, the first thing we saw was one of the man-idiots hacking wood out of doors. He was of the deaf and dumb variety, with misshapen skull; he took no notice of us, but continued at his task with curious deliberation, as if each stroke of the ax necessitated the profoundest thought. Weak in the head, obviously; but not what I call an idiot. If he could have spoken, he would doubtless have uttered as many witticisms as one hears in an English public-house at closing time. The woman was also there, sitting on the bench beside a Sister of Charity. Under-sized, stupid-looking, with mouth agape; nothing more; I have seen society ladies not unlike her in appearance. She can sew and knit stockings and even talk, they had told us. Mediocre specimens, both of them. And how about the third one, we enquired? He was working in the fields, said the Sister.

Working in the fields....

These things call themselves idiots. Even idiots, it seems, have degenerated nowadays. Mr. R. was dreadfully disappointed; and so was I. He vowed I had led him to expect something on quite another scale; and so I had. He extracted a promise, then and there, that I should show him over Valduna, the provincial lunatic asylum near Rankweil, in the hope of unearthing a few idiots worthy of the name.

Now of course you cannot have everything in this world. You cannot ask, in a district otherwise so richly endowed by Nature as this one, for the *fine fleur* of imbecility—for *crétins*. To see these marvels you must go further afield, to places like the Valtellina or Val d'Aosta (and even there, I understand, the race is losing some of its best characteristics. These doctors!) But one might at least have kept alive a specimen or two of the old school, just for memory's sake; idiots such as my sister and myself used to see, while rambling as children about these streets with the *Alte Anna*, our nurse. On that very bench, where the modish lady was reclining to-day, or its predecessor, there used to sit two skinny old madwomen side by side, with their backs to the wall. There they sat, always in the same place. They were as mad as could be, and older than the hills. A terrifying spectacle—these two blank creatures, staring into vacuity out of pale blue eyes, with white hair tumbled all about their shoulders. One of them disappeared—died, no doubt; the survivor went on sitting and staring, in her old place. There was another idiot whom we liked far better; in fact we loved him. He was of the joyful and jabbering kind, and he lived near the factory. His facial contortions used to make us shriek with laughter. Sometimes he dribbled at the mouth. When he dribbled copiously, which was not every day, it was our crowning joy.

The old Anna, of course, knew by heart every idiot within miles of our home. She specialized in such phenomena. What she liked even better was anything in the nature of an accident, operation, horrible disease, or childbirth; she knew of it, by some dark instinct, the moment it occurred: she knew! and, being forbidden to leave the children alone, dragged us with her into the remotest peasant-houses and hamlets to enjoy the sight. Above all things, she had a mania for corpses and the flair of a hyena for discovering their whereabouts. As often as there was a corpse within walking distance, she donned her seven-league boots and rushed towards it in the bee-line, carrying my sister, to save time, while I toddled painfully after. Arrived at the spot where the dead body lay, she would first cross herself and then begin to gloat. We did the same. Who knows how many maladies, how many corpses, we inspected at that tender age! A sound education. For it familiarized us with death and suffering at a life-period when one cannot yet grasp their full import; it took away, for good and all, a great part of their terrors. We were never shocked by such things; only interested—hugely interested....

After an appetizing luncheon which atoned for the bitter disappointment of this morning, we strolled upwards in the sunshine, slowly and comfortably, towards the village of Tiefis. The ancient *Dorfberg* road which started opposite the sawmill to climb the height now lies obliterated and forgotten; it was so steep that coachmen and all the rest of us—save one or other of those awesome Scotch grand-aunts, fragile and frowsy—had to get out of the carriage and walk. Here, on the upper level, stood certain immense walnut trees of ours, in whose shade I used to crawl about before I could walk. They are gone. But the distant iron target against the hill-side behind them, which served my father for rifle-practice, is in its old place; they have not troubled to pull it down. I glance into the back regions of our old house; no great change here; some of the present proprietor's children are bathing in that fountain which used to be covered with water-lilies. Then, a couple of hundred yards further on, the ochre-tinted bed of that wonderful stream which petrified leaves and grasses, a ceaseless marvel of childhood. There it is as of old, trickling downhill in the same miniature cascade. Up again, to the next level and beyond, where the forest begins and where, looking back, you have a fine view upon the Zimba.

Now these are the things for which I have come here; things for which you will vainly ransack England and the whole Mediterranean basin. You are confronted, all of a sudden, by a dusky precipice, a wall of ancient firs, glittering in the sun; their branches droop earthward in curtain-like fringes. Here the path enters the forest—an inspiring portal! To step from those bright meadows into the solemn and friendly twilight of the trees is like stepping into a vast green cavern, into another world; involuntarily one lowers one's voice. I shall be much surprised if these benign woodlands do not have a chastening influence upon the character and the whole worldly outlook of Mr. R., to whom this country and its people and language and customs are so utterly strange that he has not yet recovered from his first bewilderment; they are what he needs—what all of us need; one should return to them again and again, to breathe a cleaner air, to rectify one's perspective, to escape from the herd and the contamination of its unsteady brain.

There is a short break in the wood soon afterwards, a steep grassy slope with a hay-hut at its foot. The place is called *Hirsch-sprung*, because in olden days a hunted stag took the whole descent at a single leap. Any one who has seen stags pursued by a hound will admit that they are remarkable jumpers. They seldom get as good a chance as this, of showing what they can do. The distance aerially traversed must be about eighty yards.

Tiefis is a new and prosperous village; the old one was burnt down in the sixties. We went to my old inn where we discovered, among other things, a pretty fair-haired child, daughter of the proprietress; she has the clearest complexion imaginable and the sweetest smile, and her eyes are not blue, but of a mysterious golden-gray; the very picture of innocence, and just the kind of person to trouble desperately Mr. R., who is of the other color and at an inflammable age, though far more decent-minded than I used to be. The charm is fleeting; she will lose some of her looks; already I detect an ever so slight thickening of her throat. Goitrous throats are none too rare hereabouts and nobody seems to mind them, but Mr. R. knows nothing about such things as yet. At my invitation she came and sat down beside him, which disconcerted both of them at first, while I discussed the price of wine and other commodities with the mother, whose nervous twitch in one eye must not be mistaken for a wink. Where would it end, I enquired? Did innkeepers like herself still stock the better qualities of white, the Nieder-oesterreicher and so-called Terlaner, or red kinds like Veltliner and Kalterer See and Magdalener? Would not people, at this rate, soon give up drinking wine altogether? They were giving it up fast, she said. No peasant cared to pay 1500 kronen for a quarter of a liter. Only last week it was 800; in another fortnight it might be 2500 (it is now 4000). And so forth.

"I think it would be polite to shake hands with the little baby," said Mr. R., as we rose to depart.

"The little baby? I see. Go ahead. She won't bite."

"Of course not. But one ought to say something. What is the German for *au revoir*?"

"Say nothing to-day. Keep that for next time. Look straight into her face and smile; put your soul into it."

"I was going to do that anyhow."

Down again, by that pleasant road which connects the villages of Tiefis and Bludesch. At the foot of the hill we abandoned it and turned to the left, eastwards, up a swampy dell which, I knew, would bring us back once more to the Stag's Leap—a winding, narrow vale encompassed by woodlands and drenched, just then, in a magical light from the sunset at our back. It is called the "Eulenloch" (owl's den), and a streamlet runs down its center; the only streamlet in the district which contains crayfish and therefore used to supply us, in former days, with *potage bisque*. We captured one of these crustaceans; the brook is hereafter to be known as "ruisseau des écrevisses" (its real name is "Riedbach," from the rushes through which it flows). They dig peat here, as in many of these upland bogs, and the rank vegetation with its pungent odors, sweet and savage, has not yet been mowed down—a maze of tall blue gentians and mint and mare's-tail, and flame-like pyramids of ruby color, and meadowsweet, and the two yellows, the lusty and the frail, all tenderly confused among the mauve mist of flowering reeds. I am glad I have arrived in time to enjoy such sights; these wood-engirdled marshes have a fascination of their own. How good it is to be at home again, simmering and bubbling with contentment as you recognize the old things in their old places!

On the right flank of this owl's den there used to be a bare patch famous for its strawberries. It is now afforested and the strawberries are gone; they have strawed—strayed—elsewhere; they follow the clearings. But that hay-hut remains, that hut of the early school, built of massive timbers between which the hay comes leaking out; the roof is green with antique moss, and sulphur-hued lichen decks its beams. The architecture of these huts has undergone a change, not for the better, of late years; they are no longer squat and solid, but lanky, flimsy, and almost ignoble of aspect, though the hay within is more securely sheltered against damp by a covering of wooden boards. It is precisely this covering which spoils their appearance....

And here at last, below the Stag's Leap, is the source of the *ruisseau des écrevisses*. I knew what to expect. Those firs were cut down a good while ago, and the rivulet now wells up amid a tangle of young deciduous trees that have profited by their absence to settle down close to the brink for a season. You can hardly discover the spring for this ephemeral luxuriance; it hides itself therein like a "nymphe pudique," as Mr. R. observed. The scene was otherwise in olden days, when hundreds of mighty firs filled up all the vale. How otherwise! Then water rilled forth among their roots, a liquid joy, in the gloom of multitudinous over-arching boughs. Many are the hours I dreamt away as a lad, all alone, at this richly romantic spot. The firs will doubtless come to their rights again, and stifle in chill and darkness these sun-loving intruders; they are already planted. Would I not wait, if I could, to see the fountain as it used to be?

A short stroll late at night, down the main road towards Bludesch, in order to enjoy the scent of the fields....

I look up at my old home; it is brilliantly illuminated; three different families, they say, are at present living there. I should not care to enter that place again. Then we pass the doctor's house on our left. I tell Mr. R. of all the different village Æsculaps who have inhabited that abode; chiefly of the first one, the venerable Dr. Geiger with rubicund face and enormous goggles on his nose, who cured all my childish complaints by means of camomile tea. It was his unvarying remedy, his panacea; my mother assured me, long afterwards, that he would prescribe camomile tea, and nothing else, to pregnant women. He also had one grand and mysterious word which recurred forever in his conversation and was pronounced with a solemn face: *Abendsexacerbation*. I used to take it for abracadabra, a kind of charm, never dreaming that it meant anything. His was an original way of curing infantile headaches.

"That pain is nothing," he would remark, "I will just take it home with me," and therewith pretended to snatch up the headache and put it in his pocket. The pain always vanished— or ought to have done. I must have given him a little more trouble one day when, having been forbidden to touch the verdigris on certain copper pipes, I made a square meal of the lovely green stuff. It was a close shave, they told me afterwards; camomile worked wonders on that occasion, and during convalescence he told my mother that my pulse was placid like that of "an old cow," which it still is.

While talking of close shaves, we had reached the very spot where I had another one. No fun, driving inside that family barouche with a brace of frumpy grand-aunts—no fun at all; I therefore insisted, if one must drive, on being beside the coachman and, on that particular occasion, tumbled down from my exalted perch because the horses shied at something, and landed head first on the stony road. Ah, we are close to Bludesch now, at the ancient church of St. Nicholas; and thereby hangs another tale. It used to have windows of those small, fat, round, greenish panes of hand-made glass which were common hereabouts, till a sentimental and eccentric female relation of ours took it into her head that she would like to build a house with no other glass in its windows than these "runde Scheible"; it would be rather a gloomy sort of place inside, but so picturesque, you know! The church authorities were delighted to exchange their old-fashioned panes for others of transparent glass; so were all the peasants round about; and in briefest space of time there was not a "Butrescheibe" left in the countryside; you may see one specimen of it over the old gate at Bludenz, but this was inserted only a few years ago to give the place a more time-honored appearance. Now here again, I explain, on our return—here, immediately below my old home, stood a shrine dedicated to the Virgin. Twenty years ago, during a terrific nocturnal thunderstorm, one of those gay tumults when the sky is lilac with flashes and the Cosmos seems to be definitely cracking to pieces, it was struck by lightning. Why was it shattered, while all the neighboring houses, and even that of the unbelievers above, were spared? Nobody knows to this day. All we do know is that the priest had the débris of the disaster cleared away in record time, and another and quite insignificant structure built in its stead.

Mr. R. is not greatly moved by these and other impressive memories of my past. He prefers to extract a sort of childish fun, not for the first time, out of the shape and color of my felt hat which, being of the latest London fashion, is unfamiliar to him and therefore, in his opinion, an appropriate and inexhaustible subject for laughter in season and out of season. Young people seem to be engrossed in externals of this kind, and never to realize that a joke has its limits. I can stand as much chaff as most of us, but foresee trouble ahead unless he succeeds in discovering some fresh source of mirth.

He also thinks Tiefis a pretty village, and wants to know when we are going there again.

LUTZ FOREST

OUT of that side-valley on our east, the Walserthal,[5] issues the rushing Lutz torrent, almost a river. It joins the Ill, our main stream, a mile or so after quitting that valley; the Ill flows into the upper Rhine below Feldkirch; the Rhine into the Lake of Constance not far from Bregenz, our capital. We therefore drain into the North Sea. At a few hours' walk over the hills behind us, however, and again on the other side of the Arlberg (boundary between this province and the Tyrol), the waters drop into the Lech or Inn; this as, *via* Danube, into the Black Sea. A simple hydrographical system.

Now ever since a recent date which I forget, when the upper Rhine misbehaved itself so shockingly that the Austrian and Swiss Governments were forced to undertake some costly works with a view to ensuring better conduct in the future, our own two rivers, the Lutz and Ill, which were likewise subject to devastating floods, began to be hemmed in by stone embankments more systematically and more remorselessly than they had ever yet been in days of old, when they also gave an infinity of trouble. For it was obvious that their freakishness, coinciding with that of the Rhine and due to continued showers in these upper regions, was responsible for a certain amount of the Rhine's damage. The consequence is, that Lutz and Ill have put on new faces and grown painfully proper; they are no longer the wantons they were. And therefore all the fascinating wilderness of gray shingle and bowlders alongside, sparsely

---

[5] Professor Joseph Bergmann, in an extremely learned booklet ("Untersuchungen über die freyen Walliser oder Walser." Vienna, Carl Gerold, 1844) has proved that our Walsers, an industrious people of Burgundian stock, emigrated hitherward from the Swiss Canton Wallis (Valais) at the end of the thirteenth century and settled in this wild valley and its surroundings. It is they who brought it to its present high state of prosperity. They have kept their Swiss accent to this day, with certain idioms of their own—not every Englishman can translate "Wie tüschalat's Bobbe so schö im Pfülfli!"—and their costume is more strange than beautiful. In olden days nearly every settlement here (Bludenz, Feldkirch, Nenzing, etc.) had its own costume. There are only three left now; that of the Walserthal, the Montavon, and Bregenzerwald.

dotted with buckthorn, or white willow, or stunted little ghosts of birches—all that broad sunny desolation of their banks, where one chased crimson-winged grasshoppers and looked for garnets in those water-worn blocks of gneiss: all, all a thing of the past! Our streams now flow, in miserably straight lines, each down its own narrow channel, and large tracts of the unprofitable soil on either side have been planted with flourishing young pines and firs—an excellent investment for such worthless gravel-land hereabouts. Gone are the garnets and grasshoppers; gone is the charm of those pallid wastes. The economist gains. The poet, as usual, looks on and counts his loss.

Our village, lying on the north side of the valley, faces south; the valley may here be two and a half miles wide, as the crow flies. First come fields, then a broad stretch of woodland through which runs the Ill river and the railway Paris-Vienna, then hills once more, in the shape of the unprepossessing mountain called Tschallenga—popularly "der Stein." It is all quite simple.

On our way yesterday into these low-lying forests, we passed through the meadow beside the church of St. Anne. A large stretch of the adjoining woodland has recently been extirpated and converted into pasture—the uprooted trunks are still lying about; those two old lime trees remain untouched; the little stream has run dry. Here, on this meadow, was a surprise: a football ground. It wore a neglected air; the boys can only play on Sundays, since the war. Here the lords of Blumenegg used to be received in state by the people, their lieges; here, during the Thirty Years' War, the fighting men of the countryside were to assemble at a given signal by day or night, completely armed and furnished with three days' provision each. Here also, wholly unconcerned about the Thirty Years' War, I used to wait for a youthful companion to whom I was fondly attached; here we sat and exchanged confidences, and fashioned rustic pipes out of the twig of some shrub whose bark, in spring, can be pulled away from its wood like the glove off a finger.

On a certain occasion—an occasion which I regard as a turning-point—I happened to be all alone under the pines a little further on, near that former bank of the river which is still marked by huge blocks of defensive stone-work, now useless and smothered under a tangle of brushwood. We visited, yesterday, the very spot where, at the callow age of seven, I formulated, and was promptly appalled by its import, a far-reaching aphorism: There is no God. For some obscure reason (perhaps to test the consequences) those awful words were spoken aloud. Nothing happened. Who can tell what previous internal broodings had led to this explosive utterance! None at all, very likely. The phenomenon may have been as natural and easy of birth as the flowering of a plant, the cutting of a wisdom tooth—which, as every one knows, is nearly always a painless process. There it was: the thing had been said. Often, later on, that little incident under the pines recurred to my memory. I used to ask myself: Why make such earth-convulsing speeches? And then again: Why not? Which means the periodical relapses into credulity, into a kind of funk, rather, occurred for the next few years. After that, my intellect ceased to be clouded by anthropomorphic interpretations of the universe. Let each think as he pleases. To me, even as a boy, it was misery to profess credence in any of this Mumbo-Jumbo or to conform to any of its rites; and a considerable relief, therefore, to escape from England into a German gymnasium where, although games were not officially encouraged and work fifty times harder than at home—theology, among other subjects, being drummed into us with pestilential persistence—one was at least not asphyxiated by the noisome atmosphere of mediæval ecclesiasticism which infected English public schools in those days, and will doubtless infect them in *saecula saeculorum*. That everlasting "chapel" with its murky Gothic ritual—and before breakfast too: what a fearsome way of beginning the morning! Let each think as he pleases. I have better uses for my leisure than to try to bring others round to any convictions of mine, such as they are; far better uses. Enough for me to have watched the virus at work; and if I seem to be sensitive on this one point—why, here are scores of respectable elderly gentlemen wrangling themselves into hysterics over sanitation and Zionism and Irish politics and other conundrums that seldom trouble my dreams.

So it came about that yesterday, at the end of nearly fifty years, I approached once more, and with a kind of reverence, the sacred spot under the trees where the Lutz used to flow, and there thanked my genius for preserving me from not the least formidable of those antediluvian nightmares which afflict mankind at its most critical period of life—the nightmare of hopes never to be realized and of torments hardly worth laughing at; and from all its mischievous and perverse complications. Well, well! Men in general are brought up so differently nowadays that they cannot realize what a disheartening trial it was for some of us youngsters at that particular age and in that particular environment, where you could heave a Liddell and Scott at your form-master's head and only get a caning for it like anybody else, whereas, if you were suspected of doubting the miracle of the barren fig-tree, you were forthwith quarantined, isolated, despatched into a kind of leper-colony, all by yourself. Boys are gregarious; they resent such treatment. Let each think as he pleases. What I think is that a grown-up man would be a poor fellow, unless he felt fairly comfortable in any leper-colony into which these gentle ghost-worshipers may care to relegate him....

The woods grow thicker and more solemn as you proceed downward in the direction of Nenzing, tall firs of both varieties, some of them ivy-wreathed, interspersed with pine-trees whose trunks of rose and silver, struggling to obtain the same amount of light, shoot up straight as lances; sunny clearings and stretches of meadowland where the cattle graze knee-deep in spring; an undergrowth of junipers and other shrubs just sufficient to diversify the scene and please the eye—never too dense: noiselessly one treads on that emerald moss!

I had intended to take Mr. R. into a part of the forest which has always interested me and which I never fail to visit, a region of starved pigmy pines; and there to give him a little lecture in English on the formation of forest loam. The Lutz in 1625, or the Ill in 1651—it is impossible for me to decide which of the two—changed its course in consequence of a sudden flood and took a turn to the south, abandoning its former bed. The result was that an area of bleak shingle, far broader than the present river-bed, was left exposed in the middle of the forest. Myriads of pine seeds have been scattered upon it ever since, and the puny trees grow up slowly, dwarfishly; casting down but a yearly handful of needles each, to form the necessary soil for future generations. No moss has yet taken root after all these years, nor can the more fastidious firs draw sustenance; the little pines, rising from naked pebbles under foot, are in undisputed possession of the territory. Had there been leafy willows or alders at hand, as in the Scesa-tobel near Bludenz, the earthy covering would have been produced long ago and this quasi-sterile tract merged into the forest on either side of it. There were nothing but conifers on the spot, when the river forsook its old channel; and it is uphill work for them. The "flourishing" pines and firs of which I spoke just now have been judiciously planted; these are self-sown. They are paying for the privilege.

We also intended to visit the *Schnepfenstrich*, a piece of forest between Bludesch and Nenzing where, in days gone by, one used to lie in wait for the woodcock at nightfall. What excitement in the dim gloaming of March—*Oculi: da kommen sie*—among those patches of trees with their scent of dampness and sprouting leaves, listening for the call of the male bird and waiting to see him glide past, mysterious as a phantom! That was sport worthy of the name; though I now find it not altogether easy to conjure up the first fine rapture of that bird-massacring epoch. How unimaginative—unpoetic, let us say—are the English, who put up this apparition of the twilight in the vulgarest fashion with a dog, and then slaughter him as if he were nothing but a pheasant or partridge! Such is our manner. It is the same with the capercailzie, a stupid, worthless fowl—and worse than worthless: is he not supplanting the finer black game? Why not ennoble him in death, at least? Why not approach stealthily in the chill dusk of dawn, and espy him at last, drunk with passion, on his favorite fir? Then, if you can aim straight, he dies as we may all desire to die—swiftly, painlessly, and like a lover in his highest moment of exaltation. I know what Englishmen will say to this. They will say something about cruelty and breeding-season. Your Anglo-Saxon is always worth listening to, when he talks about cruel sports.

We had *intended*, I say; but those pests of horse-flies, which Mr. R. insists upon calling "fly-horses" or "flyses-horse," became worse and worse. There must have been cattle in this wood, not long ago. At last, despite clouds of tobacco-smoke, they drove us fairly out into the fields, and not long afterwards we found ourselves on the banks of the "Feldbächle," a cheery streamlet whose course, from start to finish, has approximately the shape of a horse-shoe or, better still, of a capital letter U, resting on its left flank. It rises in a copious and frigid fountain, soon to be visited, on the uplands behind our village, flows east through a charming swamp region, feeds the two reservoirs, tumbles downhill in a spectacular fall—the cataract whose water-power tempted my paternal grandfather to establish his cotton-mills on this spot, and which is therefore the *causa causans* of my presence here at this moment—babbles fussily through the village, and there turns westwards through these fields, to merge itself into the Tabalada stream lower down. A short but lively career.[6]

---

[6] I cannot suggest what Tabalada means unless it be what I think it is—a comical perversion of its Romansh name Aulat=*aqua lauta*, a name appropriate up to a few years ago, for it was the most crystalline water I ever saw, till we forced some of the discolored Ill to flow into it, for factory purposes at Gais. And the real name of the "Feldbächle" is Montiola-bach, which is also Latin; all that hilly region where it rises used to be called Montiola; indeed, a great number of the place-names I shall be mentioning have origin in Romansh, which is such a detestable word that I mean to call it Rhæto-Roman in future.

Our old Rhætian inhabitants, now held to be Celts and not Etruscans as certain scholars used to maintain, were defeated by Drusus and Tiberius in 15 b. c. in this very plain—so tradition says; certainly the Walgau is marked as "Vallis Drusiana" in old charts and chronicles, though another derivation is yet more plausible (see p. 152). The province was thereafter romanized, and traces of this Latin domination can be found, for instance, in those single personal names like Florentinus, Seganus, Ursicinus, which persisted hereabouts into the twelfth century; the present double family ones, of Alemannic origin, became fixed by the end of the thirteenth. As to our Rhæto-Roman names of localities—some of them speak for themselves; there is no difficulty about Scesaplana, Alpila, Fontanella, Quadera and so on, though it is rather puzzling to find a high rocky summit called "Valbona." Lutz is *lutum*, the turbid stream; Ludesch (Lodasco) stands on its banks. Bludesch was called Pludassis (*paludes*) by reason of its swampy situation. The Fön, the hot wind, is *Favonius*. Lagutz=*lacus*, a lake; which it doubtless used to be. Raggal (Roncal in chronicles), Rungalin and other such sites=*runcare*. Gamperdona=*campus rotundus*, which you will find most apposite, if you go there. Other place-names are not so easy to disentangle. Barplons=*Pratum planum*. Vanova=*Via nova*. The "Schlosstobel" at the foot of Blumenegg castle

Sometimes, in dry weather, this rivulet is blocked and allowed to flow over the parched plain. My first memory of it dates from such an occasion. There were puddles in the stream-bed here and there, puddles full of trout; and a number of Italian workmen—we employed a good many Italians at the factories—were catching these trout with their hands and eating them alive, as if they were apples. A disgusting sight, now I come to think of it.

A little later in life, I remember, and on a scorching summer afternoon, my sister and I bolted into these fields from the house, presumably after butterflies. How the sun blazed; how hot and sticky we were! And here was the old Feldbächle full of water, gadding along in its usual brisk style. An idea occurred to her. What about walking into it, clothes and all? Then, at last, we should be cool again. No; not paddle about the water like anybody else, but get right in, get properly in, in up to the neck, and lie down there as if we were in bed. A great joke. It was only on scrambling out again that we began to wonder what would happen at home and what, in fact, might be the correct thing to do under the circumstances. The problem was solved by an uphill march along the petrifying brook to far above the needful level, a flank movement eastwards in the rear of our own house, followed by a rapid descent into that of our friend the gardener who, with his usual ingenuity, lighted an immense

---

used to be called "Falster"=*Vallis torrens*. Trasseraus=*tres suors* (*sorores*). Frastafeders is simply "old Frastanz." One thing strikes me as suggestive. That Rhætians or Romans should give names to conspicuous peaks—Vallula, Zimba, Furka, Saladina: there are dozens of them—is intelligible enough. You can see a mountain from below, without climbing up. You cannot see a lake from below. Yet the names of some of our secluded Alpine waters, like Tilisuna and Formarin, whatever their origin, are not Alemannic and are therefore pre-Alemannic; which proves that these remote and inhospitable spots were already then frequented for the sake, no doubt, of their brief summer pasturage. Whence I deduce that the population of those days must have been denser than one generally imagines. Formarin, for the rest, is pronounced "Famurin" which may be "Val Murin," from the quantities of marmots (*mure montana*, contracted into our "Burmentli") up there. If this conjecture sounds far-fetched, let me hasten to say that it is not mine, but that of Max Vermunt ("Stille Winkel in Vorarlberg").

fire at which our scanty summer garments were dried, one by one.

Those old cotton-mills of ours at the foot of the cataract of which I spoke are an ugly blot on the landscape; an eyesore, none the less, which I can view without resentment, since, indirectly, I owe existence to them and would not have missed the enjoyment of this life for anything, nor would I exchange it even now for that of any other creature on earth.

The paternal grandfather who built and worked them almost to the day of his death must have been a man of uncommon grit. I know little about him. A mass of family documents full of the requisite information, as well as other papers interesting to myself, were lost in one of those accidents which occur to everybody now and then; a trunk was broken open on a journey, the clothes stolen and these letters and things scattered or thrown away by the thieves. Small comfort to receive insurance money for the clothes! I would have preferred the papers which are now lost for ever.

I cannot even say when this business was founded. It may have been in the late thirties, for he died October, 1870, aged sixty-six, at Banchory, N. B., where he ought to have died, and there lies entombed in our vault. His object in thus exiling himself and family for a whole lifetime was to earn enough money to pay back some heavy mortgages on his ancestral estate, for which he had an idolatrous affection. This much I happen to know: that in 1856 already, by working these mills, he was able to repay £36,000 towards the cost of them, and £24,000 towards redeeming the mortgages. So he set himself to his grim task; and a grim task it must have been to master the immense technical and commercial details of such an undertaking, and all in a foreign language; to import (among other little difficulties) every scrap of machinery from Lancashire with no railway nearer, I fancy, than Zurich. He worked with single aim and lived to reap his reward, although the losses due to the American Civil War, and the Austro-German one, were such that the whole enterprise nearly came to grief.[7]

His portrait in old age, engraved from a photograph on one of those shell-cameos which used to be fashionable, wears an air of clean-cut, thoughtful determination. They told me of his effective way with beggars. "Work!" he would say, whenever one of them turned up with his usual tale of misery. "Work! I also work." The other, naturally enough, professed himself quite unable to find any work. Whereupon, to the beggar's intense disgust, he promptly found it for him. These gentlemen learnt to avoid our house in his day. I also gathered that his favorite ode of Horace was "Integer vitæ." That sounds characteristic. My own fancy leans towards the Lady of Antium....

His eldest son carried on the business, and to him, with his love of mountaineering and multiple other activities, it must have been irksome in the extreme to sit in that office. He also stuck it out, but died young and, from all accounts, the best-loved man in the province, despite his Lutheran faith. Having occasion, during my last visit to Bregenz, to mention my name to an unknown shopkeeper who was to send me a parcel, I was pleased to hear him say "Your name, dear sir, is eternal in this country." It is doubtless gratifying to find yourself in a district where your family is held in honor. One must try, however, not to take these things too melodramatically. We live but once; we owe nothing to posterity; and a man's own happiness counts before that of any one else. My father's tastes happen to have lain in a direction which commended him to his fellows. Had his nature driven him along lines that failed to secure their sympathy, or even their approval, I should have been the last to complain. The world is wide! Instead of coming here, one would have gone somewhere else.

---

[7] We had our ups and downs in later times. One of the "ups" was when the factory was partially burnt some thirty years ago, and the insurance compensation enabled us not only to rebuild it on a far finer scale, but to purchase the neighboring establishment of Gais which happened to be in the market.

BLUMENEGG

AFTERNOON, and warmer than usual. Fön shifts about in irresolute, vagrant puffs of heat; the sky, shortly before sunrise, had been flaring red, copper-colored, from end to end. This is the ardent and wayward but caressing wind under whose touch everything grows brittle and inflammable; when in olden days all cooking had to be suspended and fires extinguished; when whole villages, for some trifling reason, were burnt to the ground; it was during Fön weather that Tiefis and Nüziders, and several in the Rhine valley, were annihilated within the memory of our fathers.[8] The peasants, unfamiliar with real heat, go about gasping....

While crossing our cemetery to revisit the grave of a little brother of my father's, an infant, and the Catholics were kind enough to make room for him here—it struck me how poetic are the German designations for such sad spots, *Friedhof* and *Gottesacker*, when contrasted with our soul-withering "churchyard" or "graveyard" or "burial-ground." The people hereabouts contrive to invest with a halo of romance even that most unromantic of objects, the common potato, by calling it *Erdapfel*, or *Grundbirne*. And the names of the ruined castles that strew this region, Schattenburg, Sonnenberg, Rosenegg, and so forth, were surely invented by a race that had a fine feeling for such things.

Or Blumenegg—which happens to be nothing but a translation of Florimont, the Rhaeto-Roman name of this locality.

If you follow the main road to Ludesch, you will pass through a fir wood and then come to the Lutz bridge. Do not cross the stream; keep on this side, and walk along the water. After a few hundred yards you will arrive at the "Schlosstobel" (the old "Falster"; also called "Storrbach") which rushes past the foot of Blumenegg castle. Not many years ago it descended in a wild flood, uprooting trees and covering the ground with a hideous irruption of shingle, which will remain for some little time. On the Schlosstobel's other side you enter a forest called

---

[8] The Fön, if it then existed, may be responsible for the destruction by fire of so many of the prehistoric Swiss lake settlements.

Gstinswald; part of it used to belong to our family. Here, at the entrance of this wood, stood a landmark; a picture attached to a tree, in memory of a man who was drowned at this spot while endeavoring to cross the rivulet during some spate of olden days. It was a realistic work of art, depicting both Heaven and earth. This was the subject: down below, a watery chaos, a black thundercloud out of which buckets of rain descended upon the victim whom you beheld struggling in the whirlpool of waves, while his open umbrella floated disconsolately in the neighborhood; overhead, on the other side of the thundercloud (it had taken on a golden tinge of sunshine half way through) the Mother of God with a saint or two, gazing down upon the scene with an air of detachment which bordered on indifference. The picture is no longer there; and nothing remains of its tree save a moldy stump.

From this point you can climb direct to the castle. We preferred to wander awhile up the Gstinswald which clothes the right flank of the Lutz river, in order to see what has happened to that mysterious and solitary peasant-house which lay on a grassy slope in the forest. It is still there, but those skulls of foxes and badgers and other beasts, nailed by its occupant to a certain wooden door—skulls that held a fascination for us children—are gone. And what of the snowdrops? This, and a little hillock near Ludesch, were the only places where they could be found; tiger-lilies grew elsewhere; *primula auricula* only at the Hanging Stone; cyclamen only at Feldkirch (where they were discovered in the middle of the sixteenth century by Hieronymus Bock); the cypripedium orchid (*calceolus Divæ Virginis*), the lady's slipper, at two other places; stag's horn moss, *vulgo* "Fuchsschwanz," at four or five: we knew them all! but flowers were dropped, when butterflies began. From this farmhouse you have an unexpected view upon the summit of the Scesaplana, and by far the best time to come here is after a summer shower, when a procession of white mists comes trailing out of the narrow valley, one after the other, like a troop of ghosts. Now ascend through the field and the tract of woodland immediately behind this farm, and you will reach a broad meadow which bears the old name of Quadera or Quadern; against the huge barn which used to stand there, all by itself, they have erected a modern house full of people. The castle is not far off; you must look for it, since the little path that once led up is half obliterated. And therein lies a great part of its charm; you must look for it....

When all is said and done, when you have scoured Europe and other regions in search of the picturesque and admired landscapes and ruins innumerable, that shattered old fastness of Blumenegg, up there, still remains one of the fairest places on earth. It is desolation itself, a harmonious desolation, among its dreamy firs and beeches; firs within, firs and beeches without. The roof is gone, and so are nearly all the internal partitions; nothing but the shell survives. This shell, this massive outer wall of blocks partly hewn and partly in the rough—water-worn bowlders, dragged up from the Lutz-bed below—is encrusted with moss wherever moss can grow; out of that moss sprout little firs and little beeches, drawing what nourishment they can from the old stones. They garnish the ruin. So Blumenegg is invaded by nature; and nature, here, has been left untouched. A castle in a tale! Elsewhere you see bare stretches of this wall, that tower up sadly in ever-crumbling pinnacles. All is green within the shell; its firs are so cunningly distributed that you can just see through them from one end to the other of the ruin and realize, with pleasure, that you are within some ancient enclosure. They rise out of an uneven floor whereunder, one suspects, lie buried the roof and interior walls. This floor is thickly carpeted with moss in every part. No brambles or inconvenient shrubs grow here; nothing but firs and moss, and creeping ivy, and hepatica, and daphne and the tender *Waldmeister* plant, that calls up memories of May. Once inside that green *enceinte*, a suggestion of remoteness overcomes you; the world and its jargon are left behind. There is silence save for the rushing torrent with its waterfall, three hundred feet below. In former days, this castle must have towered grandly over Ludesch and the whole valley. Viewed from down there, it now resembles an agglomeration of spiky gray crags, peering upward through the firs.

Doubtless they have written about this place and, if one took the trouble, one could learn something of its past either from archives or out of the histories published by local antiquarians. There has never been a want of such people hereabouts; the province is rich in literature of this class. A rather valuable book which has remained in my possession by a miracle and was printed in "dem Gräfflichem Marckt Embs" in 1616[9] gives some account of it; but though I know little enough, I know more than its old author could possibly have recorded, since Blumenegg "flourished" long after he did. Eight different dynasties have ruled here; the last being the Austrian Crown, to whom its rights devolved at the beginning of last century. The castle was probably built in the twelfth; it is known to have stood in 1265 and is described as a "Veste" in 1288; its lords had power over the three neighboring villages and some of the Valentschina (the old name of the Walserthal). They were answerable for their acts to no township, to no civil or religious authority whatever; to none save the Emperor himself. That is the way to live, for it was an undertaking of questionable profit to complain of such people to the Emperor. They claimed the right over life and death of their lieges and exercised it freely, "*because*"—as one of them observed in 1397—"*we possess both stocks and gallows*": an adequate reason. That is the way to talk.[10] They also executed robbers with the sword. Then, together with nearly all our feudal strongholds, this castle was sacked by the Appenzell people of Switzerland in 1405. Its outer wall is down, on the east. From this flank, presumably, the invaders entered for their work of destruction. A spot is still pointed out by the driving road, on the other side of the wild torrent, where, during some siege, the horses of a noble coach took fright at the sound of cannon-shots and threw themselves

---

[9] "Hystorische Relation," etc., of Rhetia by Johann Georg Schlehen of Rottweyl. There is a copy in the British Museum. His name is Schlee; the Schlehen on the title-page is the accusative.

[10] Justice was dispensed in sight of the gallows, the *signa meri imperi,* near the Hanging Stone (a conspicuous cliff on the Bludenz road)—dispensed upon a certain fateful meadow, the path to which used to be known as the "gallows' way," and the meadow itself "Gerichti" (Court of Justice). These names seem to have faded out of the popular memory. I like to think that the proceedings took place near that wide-branching oak, by far the finest in the district, at whose foot I used to recline in olden days. It stands between the Hanging Stone and our present railway station, opposite that detestable new cement factory, on the south side of the line. There is certainly a path leading to it from the cliff, and perhaps some dim tradition attached to this oak has saved it from the ax through all these years.

down the precipice, carriage and all.

Blumenegg revived. It was rebuilt and, during the Thirty Years' War, contained fifty Swedish prisoners in its "Keuthe," a dungeon which was pretty full even on ordinary occasions. Then, in 1650, the place was burnt down with all it contained— priceless treasures among them, such as the long-hidden manuscript of the *Chronicon Hirsaugiense* in the handwriting of its famous author, the Abbot Tritheim, of which, fortunately, a copy had been taken a little earlier at St. Gallen. The building was reduced to ashes a second time in 1774, and thereafter allowed to fall into ruin, for ever. Why, I cannot say. Who would live at Blumenegg if he could, particularly in that earlier period? The south part of the castle, facing the valley, bears traces of a clumsy reconstruction. It lacks the dreaminess of the remaining part; a harsher element of stones dominates in this quadrangle, and you can discover an old fire-place with blackened chimney and a few projecting wooden beams. For the rest, it must have looked well, blazing up there; I can picture the villagers of Ludesch down below, watching the conflagration and dancing with joy!

It did not take us long to make ourselves comfortable within the enclosure, on that soft carpet. The sun was still fairly high; it percolated through the fir-branches, etching lively patterns all around us; it drew luscious tints, of unearthly brightness, out of the deep green moss. And here we stayed, and stayed. We had fallen under the spell of the place and neither felt inclined to move; some drowsy genius hovered in our neighborhood. It was so warm and green; so remote. How one changes! I used to find it irksome to be obliged to show this castle to friends or relatives. Left to my own devices, I avoided the place; there were no butterflies, no fossils, no snakes, no birds, worth mentioning. Ten to one, not even a squirrel....

Since then, castle-ruins galore have been inspected. Europe is studded with them. I think of those absurd places in England or on the Rhine, possibly restored and in every case sullied by tourists and their traces; out of them, the spirit of romance has been driven beyond recall. The frowning rock-fortresses of the Bavarian Palatinate—Dahn, Weglenburg, Trifels, Madenburg, Lindelbronn, Fleckenstein: how one used to know them!—are in better case, or were, thirty odd years ago; even they have not escaped contamination. Certain southern ruins are no doubt imposing; but bleak. Bleak! Mere piles of masonry, they have not been hallowed by lapse of years; they lack the refinement which verdure alone can give; their ravages will show for all time. Those ravages are healed here; trees and moss have done their work so well that an exquisite *tonalité* pervades the spot. Blumenegg is all in one key. Men have left it to crumble alone; and alone it crumbles, slowly and graciously, to earth. Nothing and nobody intrudes, save the wild things of nature; you must look for it. A much-frequented path—short cut from the Walserthal to the railway-station—runs close by; who ever steps aside? Resting in that enchanted penumbra, one gains the impression that Blumenegg is neither sad nor smiling; a little wistful, a little sleepy, like old Barbarossa in his cave.

What of the intimate, domestic life of its former occupants? On a night, say, of December, 1402—of whom did the family consist, what was their costume, their dinner menu, the sound of their dialect, their theme of conversation? Does it help us much to know that Count Wolfart, familiarly termed "the wolflet"—it probably suited him—could bring five thousand men into battle? (An enormous number; can they have meant five hundred?) Poke our noses, as we please, into chronicles, and pore over books like Freytag's "Bilder aus der deutschen Vergangenheit," these men remain crepuscular, elusive shapes. The Romans of the Empire, the pyramid builders of Egypt, move in comparative daylight before our eyes....

Meanwhile the mossy floor has ceased to glow. Slanting sunbeams come filtered, lemon-tinted, through the beech-leaves out there; they spatter the fir-trunks with moon-like discs and crescents. And still we refuse to budge. A soft tinkle of cow-bells, inaudible by day, floats up from the valley; even as we look on, those silvery patches begin to fade from the trees, and everything trembles in the witchery of dusk. Interplay of light and shade is ended. We feel no change, while darkness creeps up stealthily; only the voice of the torrent has grown louder and hoarser. A flock of crows suddenly arrives, with the evident intention of roosting above our heads. Something apparently is not in order to-night, for they rise again with discontented croakings. No wonder. Mr. R. has been lying flat on his back for the last half hour immediately below them, playing tunes on that mouth-organ—that talisman which I, in a moment of inspiration, presented to him. On such occasions he is lost to the world and in a kind of trance; one arm beats time in the air. The birds cannot possibly see him, but they can hear the music, and no crow on earth, not the wisest old raven, could guess the names of the "morceaux" which have just been performed.

"What were you playing, all this time?" I enquire, during a pause.

"Well, there was the *marche des escargots*, which you must be sick of, by now—a fine piece, all the same; and the old *vache enragée*——"

"I know. Rather noisy, the old *vache*."

"What do you expect? Do you want her to go mad in her sleep. Then the *fantaisie* of last week, and *pluie dans les bois*, and the duet between two sea-nymphs, and *rêve d'un papillon* and a new one, a little caprice or something, which has not yet got a name. I am thinking of calling it *coin des fleurs* (Blumenegg[11])."

Strange! This instrument appeals, as I expected, to certain primitive and childlike streaks in his nature. At first, needless to say, it was thrown aside with contempt; then shyly picked up from time to time. Now the two are inseparable; it accompanies him everywhere in a specially built leather case, and I should not be surprised to learn that he takes it to bed with him. As to these "morceaux"—they have a real interest, seeing that Mr. R. knows nothing whatever of music, cannot remember a tune, never whistles or sings, and has only a feeble ear for rhythm in poetry. None the less, each of these *melodies* possesses a character of its own and, once invented, never varies by a note. Their names, I understand, are recorded in his diary. They are worth it.

Night; and dark night, under these trees. The Fön is over, a chill dew has fallen. We rise at last, rather stiff, and proceed cautiously downwards till we reach the path; then across the bridge and into the open meadow, the so-called fox-meadow, when—our match-box, our only match-box: where is it gone?

---

[11] I have just discovered, rummaging among some old papers, a musical composition by my mother entitled "Blumenegg." It is dated October, 1861; three years before her marriage.

Forgotten inside the castle, on the moss. Back again, to crawl about on hands and knees till the precious object has been found; then once more to the fox-meadow. So we wander homeward, in full content. The dew-drenched field sends a pleasant shiver up through our boots, and a chorus of crickets is chirping lustily in its damp earth. Stars are out; the Tschallenga hill, confronting us, has become pitch-black; those Rhætian peaks are like steel, and their snow-patches have a dead look at this hour. Tawny exhalations, as of lingering day, flit about the Swiss mountains on our west. Some grass has been mown up here, during the hot afternoon; the air is full of its fragrance.

Blumenegg and such places—these are the surroundings in which children ought to grow up. At home, domestic beasts of every kind, and gardens and orchards; further afield, flowery meadows and forests; the glittering snow of winter and cloudless summer skies; rock and rivulet; a smiling patriarchal peasantry all about; these are the surroundings. Keep them off the street-pavement.

Impermanent things, like pavements and what they stand for, stimulate the adult; they overstimulate children, who should be in contact with eternities. In a town you may watch the progress of their warping; how they grow up precocious and partially atrophied; defrauded of their full heritage as human beings. Indeed all town-bred persons, with the rarest exceptions, are incomplete, in a certain small sense of that word. They show a gap which, unlike other gaps (deficient learning or manners) can never be filled up in later years. The intelligent countryman does not take long to appreciate the most complex wonders of civilization, because his life began at the right end of things; your citizen will only stare at those other wonders with more or less impatience: he began at the wrong end. One can tell after five minutes' conversation whether a man has been brought up in city or country, for no townsman, be he of what class he pleases, can hide his native imperfection.

Or go to literature, the surest test, since *scripta manent*. It happened to be my fate for some years to peruse daily a considerable mass of the latest so-called lyric poetry, and a melancholy task it was following these youngsters as they floundered about in a vain search after new gods, unaware of the fact that the lyrical temper demands a peculiar environment for its nurture, that gods are shy, and not to be encountered in music-halls and restaurants, or even during a week-end at the seaside. There were no eternities for these people, and consequently no true joy, no true grief; no heights, no depths; they fell into two categories: the hectic and the drab. The lyrical temper.... One uses such expressions, without perhaps being clear as to their meaning. What is the lyrical temper? A capacity to warble about buttercups? I should describe it as a sympathetic feeling for the myriad processes of nature, and the application of this gift towards interpreting human phenomena with concision and poignancy; the sense, in short, of being borne along, together with all else on earth, in a soft pantheistic commotion.

That is a view of life which generates both tears and smiles, and one which you will vainly seek in any town-bred writer. Compare Milton, not with Theocritus or Shakespeare, but with a poet of the caliber of Ovid, and you will realize how much more individual and authoritative his utterance would be, had he enjoyed Ovid's advantages in childhood. He saw nature through books, say Mr. Tuckwell and Mr. Cotterill and all the rest of them;[12] his scenery is charmingly manufactured according to the renaissance prescription, and if you know your Italian poets you can tell beforehand what Milton will have to say; a master of landscape arrangement, without a doubt, but— he lacked what Ovid possessed, an æsthetic personality; he was a moralist, as every one grows to be, who takes his fellow-

---

[12] The former of these speaks of Milton's "habitually loose botany." No great blemish; given the themes he loved, it might be argued that much of Milton's peculiar aroma would evaporate, had he been meticulous in such details like Tennyson or de Tabley. Theocritus is hard to catch napping; but Ovid, for example, tells us that *buxus* grows on Mount Hymettus. There is no box on Hymettus, though it prospers in certain gardens of Athens (e. g., the Crown Prince's); Ovid was thinking of the dwarf holly. It is the worst of writing poetry, that you are apt to be torn between respect for truth and the exigencies of scansion. What would the painfully correct Lucretius have done with this *buxus*?

creatures at their own estimate. And how avoid doing this, if you are always among them? For there they live clustered together, and involuntarily disposed to attach undue significance to themselves and their works, to lose their sense of proportion, until some little interference from that despised exterior makes itself felt, an earthquake or such-like, which gives these posturing ephemerals an opportunity to straighten out their values again.

Charles Lamb is another street-walker, and one whose relish of man and his ways, to my taste, never cloys, inasmuch as it remains firm-fixed on the hither side of lachrymosity. Yet is there not a certain shallowness in his preoccupation with fellow-creatures? Shallowness suggests want of depth; want of breadth is what I wish to imply. Zest, temperamental zest, should be a fountain, scattering playfully in all directions; Lamb's comfortable variety is unilateral—a fountain gushing from a wall. How many avenues of delight are closed to the mere moralist or immoralist who knows nothing of things extra-human; who remains absorbed in mankind and its half-dozen motives of conduct, so unstable and yet forever the same, which we all fathomed before we were twenty! Well, their permutations and combinations afford a little material for playwrights and others, and there is no harm in going to the theater now and then, or reading a novel, provided you have nothing better to do.

FATHER BRUHIN

THIS was a pious pilgrimage.

Ages ago there used to come to our house a visitor, a friend of my father's, a Benedictine monk of the name of Bruhin. Of him I have, or till yesterday thought to have, dim, childish memories. He lived in the neighboring convent of St. Gerold— offshoot of the famous Einsiedeln—and was a naturalist, a *rara avis* hereabouts. I still possess seven of his papers, mostly on the fauna and flora of this particular province: thoroughly good work. He was a loving and accurate student both of animals and plants, and of their literature. St. Gerold is the second of various hamlets and villages in the long verdant Walserthal on our east, up which now runs a convenient carriage road ending (the road; not the valley) at the distant Buchboden, five hours' march away. We went there, because I was anxious to learn, if possible, a few details of Bruhin's life and to see whether their library contained any other works by him.

It is a pleasant, easy walk to St. Gerold, but the pilgrimage proved a disappointment. In the Prior's absence, the archives could not be consulted; a young monk, a stranger who was undergoing a kind of rest-cure here—he looked a little haggard—accompanied us up to the library at the top of the building. It was well stored with books such as one might expect to find there, but contained not a scrap by Bruhin.

At the library our guide left us in charge of that old woman who has haunted the premises from time immemorial; her hair has grown whiter since last we met, her eyes are black as ever. She showed the way through some of those comfortably furnished bedrooms with their fine seventeenth century wood-carvings; into the church, which has been tastefully redecorated and where the recent governmental brigandage has not spared even the greater of the tin organ-pipes; finally down to the kitchen which, like the organ, is worked by electricity. There she fed Mr. R. on cider and cheese, saying she hoped they would soon be able to receive guests again and keep them overnight, if necessary; at present, everything was upside down, everything!

Had the Prior been visible, our search might have led to something; he was away on the mountains. Whether he resembles him of olden days? That one, I remember, used to come down and see us, and could generally be induced to stay for luncheon or dinner. It was his habit, while eating, to produce a formidable smacking noise—Germans call it *Schmatzen*—with his lips, a noise which we were strictly forbidden to make. One day at mealtime I gave a splendid imitation of the Prior over his soup, thinking that what was good enough for him would surely be good enough for me, and hoping, at all events, to gain some little applause. Instead of that, I was told: "Only His Reverence the Prior may make that noise. When you are Prior, you shall make it too. Meanwhile, try to eat like everybody else, unless you want to be sent out of the room." A damper....

So much for Bruhin. All we gleaned at St. Gerold was that he served as "Co-operator" there from 1865 to 1868 and after that, presumably, left the convent. If so, the monk whom I hazily recall must have been a different one, unless Bruhin continued his visits to us from some other quarter after 1868. The Bregenz libraries might contain more of his writings; I shall look for them, if we go there.[13]

Homewards again. On leaving one of those wooded torrents that seam the road, a little incident was recalled to my mind by the sight of a certain wayside shrine which stands here. We were once passing along, as children, when we noticed that its door had been left open and a heap of coppers laid inside by some pious person or persons for the benefit of any poor travelers who might care to help themselves. I imagine it was my sister's idea. She took a handful, and persuaded me to take one too. Nobody saw us; the governess was walking on ahead. She behaved even more flagrantly on another occasion when a

---

[13] Professor K. W. von Dalla Torre mentions him in his "Zoologische Literatur von Tirol und Vorarlberg bis inclusive 1885." He enumerates eighteen different monographs by him, dealing with the fauna alone of this province. (His botanical works are more important.) He also notes that Bruhin is "at present (1886) in Columbus, Ohio, U. S. A." It is a far cry to Ohio! If he stayed there any length of time, he is sure to have made a name for himself. He always signs himself "Th. A."; Dalla Torre calls him "Theodor," which is probably correct; in the list of subscribers to Heer's "Urwelt der Schweiz" (1865, p. xviii) he figures as "Thomas."

plateful of money was being held aloft, for the same charitable purpose, among a congregation pouring out of some church. She reached up and swiftly grabbed a number of coins; perhaps I followed her example. Now what could we children want with money? The delicacies of the village were only three: sugar-candy in crystals, dried figs strung together, and black sticks of licorice (*vulgo* "Bährendreck") and we had exhausted their charm long, long ago, in the days of the old Anna.

This nurse it was, by the way, who first took me to the hamlet of Thüringerberg, where I now found myself walking with Mr. R. who had induced me, for reasons which became apparent later on, to abandon the main road in favor of one that leads due west. It shows how little she then knew the country—she was a Tyrolese, not a native—that, after dragging me up here, aged three or four, she had to enquire the name of the place. I came home with a wonderful tale of having been to Thüringerberg, which was not believed; old Anna, afterwards, got it hot for making me walk too far. Up there, meanwhile, the kindly priest invited us to his house to rest; he gave us coffee and honey, and even offered me a pinch of his snuff—the first of several I have since taken.

Two roads descend from Thüringerberg in the direction of the distant Satteins—the convenient new one down below, and the ancient track on the higher level. Of course we chose the latter, that old, grass-grown, abandoned path. Memories lurk about these forsaken places; and memories have become my hobby during the last week or so. This particular track reminds me of sundry strolls down here ages ago with a Sempill cousin, the jovial Jumbo, who turned up in this country at odd intervals to our infinite delight. He was so utterly different from all the other people who arrived from those remote regions! The peasants adored him; he could hold long conversations with them in their own language by imitating the sound of their voices, which amused them mightily; he knew not a word of German. He used to sit for hours in their orchards, drinking wine or playing with the babies; when any one greeted him on the road with the usual "Grüass Gott," he would reply "Great Scot"; if they said "Gueta Tag," he said "Good dog." What a relief was Jumbo, after those legions of unspeakable grand-aunts! They never left us alone; they were always pulling us about, as if we had no nurses or governesses of our own, to teach us how to behave. Always interfering! You mustn't eat this; you mustn't do that; little girls don't climb trees; little boys ought to know that cows are not made to be ridden about on; never jump down till the carriage stops; you know what happened to Don't Care? He was hanged; have you said your prayers? Children should be seen and not heard; a fourth helping? Now don't do yourself any violence, dear; it's long past bed-time—how we loathed the entire clan! Nearly everything, in fact, that hailed from Scotland was fraught with terrors.

But the terror of terrors was our paternal grandmother. If the others of that family resembled her, their descendants are to be pitied. And to think that she may have been the best of all of them! I confess that, looking over some photographs at this distance of time, I fail to see anything terrible in her appearance; here she is, for instance, at Llandudno, looking straight at you, grave and serene, with the long upper lip peculiar to her family and a high forehead; rather a handsome old woman, and one who evidently knows her mind. That may well be. Handsome or not, she spanked me as an infant, before I could walk—so much I remember clearly; what I cannot clearly remember is, whether she had any plausible reason for doing it. Later on, she punished us in the stern judicial manner which was agreeable to the taste of her generation and which is precisely the one way children should never be punished. Wonderful tales were told us of her methods of subduing her only daughter, who died in youth—perhaps from the effects of it—and lies buried under an elaborately inscribed tombstone in the Protestant cemetery at Rome. No doubt she meant to do right; it is an old pretext for doing wrong. Children should be "broken": that was her theory.

She never broke me. Something else happened one day, during the Christmas holidays in England. I was in my twelfth year, all alone, perfectly comfortable and perfectly well, delighted to have escaped for a season out of some absurd school, and reading the "Mysteries of Udolpho" in the library when the old thing entered with an all-too familiar silver tray, bearing the abominable mixture known as "Gregory's Powder." It was her universal remedy for every complaint of mine, from a sprained ankle to a toothache, the principle being that, whatever might be amiss, Gregory's Powder, by virtue of its villainous taste alone, must inevitably do good, if not as a medical preparation, then as an incitement to humility and obedience. This filthy poison I had hitherto swallowed like a lamb; and been made duly ill in consequence. On that particular occasion, however, the sight of the tray stirred me as never before; all the accumulated bile of similar torments in the past surged up; it was my first experience of "seeing red." Guided by a righteous demon of revolt, I seized a stick which stood in a corner at my elbow—an elaborate concern of hippopotamus-hide with carved ivory top, which some good-for-nothing uncle had brought from Natal—and therewith knocked the tray out of her hand and then went for her with such a dash that she fled out of the room. It happened in the twinkling of an eye. I knew not how the thing was done; it was plain, now, what people meant when they said that So-and-so was "not responsible for his actions." On mature deliberation I decided, in the very words of the old lady, that *all was for the best*. There was an end of Gregory's Powder. That is the way to treat grandmothers of this variety. She dared not tackle me; she was too old and I too tough, being then in the habit of winning most of the gymnastic prizes at school. As always before, she had tried to impose upon me by sheer strength of personality, and suddenly, for the first time, found herself confronted by a new and persuasive argument—brute force.

Well! To attack your grandmother with a walking-stick is not polite. On the other hard, there is no reason why boys should be needlessly tortured; they suffer quite enough, as it is. If I had not acted as I did, she would have continued to poison me with the stuff to the end of her long life. Why suffer, when you can avoid it? And there I leave this ethical problem. For the rest, in her heart of hearts, she was perhaps not quite so "surprised and grieved" (a favorite phrase of hers, like "I sincerely hope and trust") as she professed to be; so strong was her family sense that she may well have been charmed with this premature exhibition of ancestral savagery; maybe she was anxiously waiting for it to appear, and chose Gregory's Powder as a kind of test or provocative. If so, it worked. One thing is certain: referring to the episode, she told another of those old women, who repeated it to me long afterwards, that I was plainly the son of my father—good news, so far as it went....

Phantoms!

Meanwhile we wandered along that ancient track towards the sunset, with the spacious Ill valley at our feet, and on its further side, the Rhætikon peaks which had grown more imposing in proportion as we ourselves had mounted upwards. On these slopes they were gathering the cherries with ladders; diminutive fruit on enormous trees. Here are also wild maples, those pleasant Alpine growths that clamber down from their homes overhead and indulge in a tasteful habit of clothing trunk and branches in a vesture of dusky green moss. The wood is so white that it is used—the nearest approach to ivory—for fashioning the sculptured images of the Crucified which one sees everywhere. The fairest maple in the whole district is that which forms a landmark on the path between Raggal and Ludescherberg; you can see it from the other side of the Walserthal, three miles off.

Presently we found ourselves in one of those narrow dells common hereabouts, dells that run parallel to the main valley, east and west; they may be due to ice-action in the past. It is curious, in such places, to observe how the plants select their aspect according to whether they relish sunshine or not; there are two different floras growing within twenty yards of each other. Here, on our left, gushes out a noble spring; it accompanies us, forming a succession of flowery marshes. They are still there—the bulrushes in the last of its hill-girdled swamps; this is one of the three places where bulrushes can be found. Thereafter you pass that peasant's house, solitary and prosperous—what winter landscapes must be visible from its windows!—and enter the wood. Our path, once well trodden, is now hard to follow. It begins to lose itself——

Ah, and the old woman's mania against tobacco; I had nearly forgotten this. It was sincere, like all else in her nature, yet incredible in its intensity. Somewhere about the fifties she ordered a pair of boots from the local man, under the condition that he was not to smoke while making them. They arrived. "That man has smoked!" she declared, and refused to accept them; she knew from their smell that he had broken his agreement (of course he had). This legend was still current here in the nineties. Up in Scotland, despite the visitors, she never allowed a smoking-room to be built. We were not permitted to smoke even in the grounds. A military cousin, a distinguished man, was told that if he wished to smoke after dinner he could walk to the end of the drive, and indulge his low tastes on the main road. My sister used to shoulder her rod and go "fly-fishing" at the most improbable hours and seasons of the year, solely in order to be able to enjoy her cigarette in peace.

She expired in grand style, up there. We were chamois-shooting at Lech, not far from here,[14] when a message came to the effect that she was at the point of death. We packed up and rushed to the Highlands, losing a whole day at Calais because the boats could not run on account of a storm. On our arrival, the doctor said, "She ought to have been dead four days ago." None the less, she had made up her mind not to depart till everything was in order. She went through her will, clause by clause. Was there any objection to this or that? Had she done the right thing by So-and-so? Or had she perhaps forgotten anything? It was all in perfect order, we assured her. She gave us a fine old-fashioned blessing, and was dead a few hours later....

And now we were threading our way through a veritable tangle, a branch-charmed tangle, and the light overhead grew dimmer. A golden suspense was brooding over the forest. How sweet, how *intimate*, are these hours of late afternoon under the trees, when all is voiceless and drowned in mellow radiance; how they conjure up sensations of other-where, and cleanse the

---

[14] We generally went to Lech in threes. Now the inn at Lech was not a bad one; so good indeed, that its praises have been sung by no less an authority than the writer Ludwig Steub, who was also a frequent visitor at our house in times gone by. But our own cuisine and cellar were still better, and accordingly we were wont to take up by cart a vast store of provisions, only sleeping at the inn and occasionally ordering some little dish or a quarter of wine for the sake of appearances. To recoup himself, the innkeeper used to charge us so preposterously for these trifles that on one occasion we had a solemn row with him and refused to pay. He yielded. Not long afterwards there was printed in some local paper a spirited poem in the mock-heroic style, with the refrain:
Die Heiligen Drei Könige, mit irrendem Stern—
Die essen und trinken, und zahlen nicht gern!
I wish I had kept a copy.

miry places of the mind!

A few years hence, and every trace of this old path will have vanished. It ended, for us, in a kind of gulley; the gulley ended in the new road lower down. And where did the new road end?

Where else, but at Tiefis?

The mention of Llandudno reminds me that I may have been unfair to that old grandmother. For I knew full well that she detested places like Llandudno or Clifton or Cheltenham, and yet she would take us there for the Easter holidays at our own request, in order that we might gratify a taste for fossils; which is surely to her credit. Not every grandmother would have made such a sacrifice for two objectionable boys. As a set-off to this, however, I must record that she used to make me play Wagner to her, much against my will—an inexplicably modern trait of hers, this love of Wagner, and all the more singular since he, at that time, was accounted a dangerous lunatic. (Perhaps she only asked me to play because at such moments, at least, I could not be up to any other devilry.) She also insisted on our both reading "Marmion" aloud; partly because it was her dear dead husband's favorite poem, and partly on account of a family legend to the effect that certain of its cantos were composed on our property. Can that have improved its flavor?

"Marmion" we thought dreadful rot. To revenge ourselves, we made a farce of these recitals, by going through the lines in a toneless voice and laying stress not where the poet and common sense meant it to lie, but on that precise syllable where, by the structure of the verse, it came to lie; let any one read a page of "Marmion" according to this recipe, and note the rich and unforeseen results! It was only by a miracle that we managed to keep our countenance; or rather, not by a miracle at all, but by a systematic education in the art of "not exploding." The old lady writhed and squirmed under this outrage upon her divine Sir Walter, but said never a word; gulping down her discomfort with the same air of dour determination with which, at dinner, and solely to set us a good example, she gulped down indigestible fragments of plum-pudding, roly-poly and other hyperborean horrors glistening with suet, although well aware that such things are not fit for human consumption. Of course we were obliged to gulp them down too, with this difference, that she had Madeira and port to wash the taste out of her mouth, while we only got claret, which made it worse. What a life!

RAIN

RAIN once more....

"Now this is the *comble*," said Mr. R. this morning, entering my room with a pair of boots in his hand.

"What's up?"

"Look!"

They had inserted new laces, without having been asked to do anything of the kind.

Every day, and all day long, similar little experiences are thrust upon him; he has lived in a state of chronic amazement since his arrival. That is not surprising. His acquaintance with the life of taverns has been confined to those of Italy and of France; the unpunctuality and brawling of the one, the miserliness and thinly veiled insolence of the other—the general discomfort of both. "Nobody will believe me," he says, "when I tell them how one lives in these villages. Fortunately I have my diary."

Our bill of fare has varied with every meal; only once were they obliged to apologize for giving us the same meat, venison, on two days running, and even then it was prepared differently. With the exception of *Hasenpfeffer*—close season for hares till 1st of September—we have gone through that entire list of local delicacies, and thereto added several more.

These people really make one feel at home. There is an all-pervading sense of peace and plenty, of comfort, in a word; not discomfort. Everything is in order, and the place so clean that you could dine on the floors. The household works like a well-oiled machine—if you can imagine a machine that wears throughout its parts a perennial smile. Kindliness is the tone of this house; of the whole village; of all these villages. It does one good to live among such folk. It is doing Mr. R. more good than he imagines. He begins to realize what is hard to realize in Mediterranean countries: that men can be affable and ample, and yet nowise simpletons. Match-boxes given away gratis; beefsteaks that you cannot possibly finish; four vegetables to every course of meat; electric lights burning night and day; fresh towels all the time; apples and pears thrown to the pigs; mountains of butter and lakes of honey for breakfast—in fact, a system of wanton *gaspillage* that would send a French housewife into epileptics. All this, I tell him, is the merest shadow of what was. And among the numerous visitors to our inn there is never a harsh word; no sullenness, no raised voices, no complaints. We hear the house door being shut down below, every night, amid cheery talk and laughter.

Yet three out of five village taverns are closed—disastrous symptom, among so convivial a people. The depreciation of the currency.... There are men, respectable men, who have not tasted a drop of wine for the last year, which is a shameful state of affairs. Only factory hands and such-like can afford to pay the present price of 8000 kronen for half a liter. Less than that sum, namely 7000, was what our tailor gave for his two-storied house with a garden and field. We watched a pig-auction the other day (where else, but at Tiefis?). A young one, weighing about seventy pounds, went for 610,000 kronen. In olden days, they would have made you a present of him.

The peasants are particularly hard hit this year. Our valley has always been celebrated for its fertility, the result of age-long tillage and manuring, and whoever walks to-day about those cultivated fields, ignorant of their normal condition, might think that these crops of hay, wheat, maize, tobacco (every one may plant his own tobacco; the trouble begins, when you try to make it smokable), beans, hemp, flax, potatoes, cabbage, beetroot, poppies, pumpkins and what not, look sufficiently thriving. That is a mistake. The fruit-harvest promises well; these fields are in a bad way. The *Engerlinge*, the larvæ of the cockchafer, have been unusually active of late. This miserable worm which lives underground, gnawing away the roots, had hitherto been kept in its place by the moles. But during the war and afterwards moles were destroyed as never before, for the sake of their skins. A mole eats one and a half times its own weight every day; he prefers the *Engerlinge* to all other food. So the larvæ now thrive, because the war was responsible for the death of the moles. One result of the war, so far as this little economic byway is concerned.

Other results. A favorite method of preventing damage by *Engerlinge* is to kill the cockchafer itself. They used to be murdered by myriads, either while flying about at night, or in the early morning when they cling, weary and drunk with dew, to the trees. Boys would do this for a trifling sum, or for the fun of the thing. They are too busy nowadays; they must do the work of those who were killed. And of those who have free time on their hands, the decent ones refuse the job because they are ashamed to ask the prices now ruling (and their fathers will not let them take less); the others demand so much that the peasant cannot pay them. Our village elders have done their best to face the mischief. They have decided that every land-owner must bring in a certain measure of cockchafers or deposit a certain sum of money; whoever collects more than this stipulated measure, is paid extra out of the sum deposited by the others; whoever fails to come up to the standard, is fined in proportion. The provincial government has also forbidden the destruction of moles, and to-day's paper, now lying before me, contains an eloquent article entitled "Spare the moles!"

It is too late. The village of Bratz (=*pratum*), for example, is so sorely tried by the plague of these larvæ that a rich peasant owning, let us say, six cows, will not be able to cut enough fodder to keep them alive through the winter; his crop of hay is too impoverished. What shall he do? He is in the dilemma of seeing a couple of his beasts perish from starvation, or of selling them at their present value, although fully aware that by the time spring comes round and fodder is again plentiful, he will not be able, with the same amount of money, to purchase even a quarter of a cow to eat his grass; so rapid is the depreciation of the currency.

In this and other matters the peasantry, the backbone of the province, is being systematically ruined. The blow was undeserved. They were dragged into this tragic farce through no fault of their own, and are now paying for the folly of others. True, they revenge themselves on the rich factory hands and bureaucrats; they charge fantastic prices for milk and other agricultural products. The others retaliate by burning their hay-huts. There was a good deal of incendiarism in the Bludenz district last winter. Mutual ill-will is the result. And their so-called betters, the *rentiers* who, after a life of drudgery in office or elsewhere, laid aside sufficient money to build themselves a house wherein to end their days, are in still more pitiable plight. Such is the case of an old gentleman of my acquaintance at Bludenz, who had worked from the age of fourteen till after seventy, and had been able to acquire what seemed a considerable fortune. What are even a million kronen to-day? And how is he to earn more, at the age of eighty-six?

Industrial workmen, no doubt, are doing uncommonly well; that English eight hours' nonsense fosters their pretensions, and as often as they consider their pay insufficient, they go on strike and obtain more. The bureaucrats also thrive in a lesser degree. There is an employee to every five men in this country; a scandalous plethora, but who would not be an employee—one of the few careers whereby a native, under existing circumstances, may hope to escape starvation? So do we foreigners. For apartments, lighting, laundry, repairs to clothes and boots, food which for excellence and variety would be unprocurable, pay what you please, in any English village five times the size of this one, for as much wine, beer, *schnapps* and cider as we can hold we pay a sum which works out, for both together, at three shillings a day. This includes an additional 10 per cent on the total, which I insist upon paying for service, though it cost some little argument before I could make them accept it. Such are the results of the "Valuta," so far as Englishmen are concerned.

Valuta: that is one of three words which you may now for the first time hear repeated from mouth to mouth. The other two are "Anschluss" and "Miliz." These matters have been adequately discussed in our own Press; I will only say, as regards the last of them, that no government, however wise and well-intentioned, can enforce its wishes if you take away its means of doing so: a militia. One does not expect high-priced inter-allied experts to be equipped with either sympathy or imagination; that would be asking too much. They should, at least, possess a little common sense and knowledge of history. Western Europe, scared to death of bolshevism in Russia, is busily engaged in manufacturing it elsewhere; and if this once gentlemanly province now exhales, as does the rest of the country, a strong reek of communistic fumes, it is our experts who are to blame. Ah, well! When the broth is boiling, the scum invariably rises to the top and stays there, until some businesslike *chef* comes along, to cream off this filthy product and throw it down the drain.

Valuta: wondrous are its workings. There is hardly an ounce of butter procurable in Bludenz, which is enclosed in grazing grounds. Where has it all gone? Over the mountains, into Switzerland. Valuta! Your Austrian smuggler is delighted; he receives five times the price he would get if he sold the stuff in his own country, and in Swiss money too, which may have doubled in worth by the time he reaches home again. Your Swiss buyer is delighted; he pays less than half the price he would have to pay for his own product. The local poor suffer, meanwhile, especially the children; for the nutritive value of butter, in the shape of *Schmalz*, is great, and this condiment used to figure in all their principal dishes, and would be doubly needful now that meat is quite beyond their reach. Altogether, these children—a shadow seems to have passed over them, witnessing the distresses of their parents. They are paler than they used to be, and graver of mien; far too many are insufficiently clad and unshod. An Englishman might think ten shillings a reasonable price for a pair of sound children's boots; the native cannot afford 110,000 kronen, a sum for which formerly he could have bought half a village. Even the post-boy, a lively youngster who happens to be a grandson of that old gardener of ours, presents himself up here every morning without shoes or stockings. He has none.

I glance, for further informative matter, down the columns of that paper which bids us "Spare the moles!" and observe that it contains, among its advertisements, an offer by a furrier of two hundred kronen for each moleskin brought to him. This does not sound as if the provincial government's decree were being enforced very drastically. The same gentleman is ready to pay exactly a thousand times as much for the skin of pine martens, which can be worth little enough at this warm season of the year. The animal is of the greatest scarcity in our neighborhood.[15]

---

[15] I knew an old hunter of Ludesch who claimed to have killed seventy-five pine martens near that village. I have seen only two in my whole life hereabouts; and not a single one within the last thirty-five years, despite never-ending rambles among these forests. But we had a pair of beech martens under the eaves of our house, which they reached by climbing along the branches of a mighty walnut tree that leaned over the roof. In the daytime they were never to be found. By night they made such a din of scuttling and scampering that visitors, sleeping in rooms below, had to be warned of their existence.

And here is a final, thrilling item. The midwives of Feldkirch, assembled in conclave, have regretfully decided that the charges for attendance are to be doubled in future.

Midwives, I suspect, are not the only professional ladies who have lately been obliged to raise their tariff.

Towards nightfall, a gleam of sunshine after the rain. Out for a stroll, after dinner....

They have anointed our boots with badger's fat, in case we traverse any wet fields. We are only going along the main road towards Ludesch. That bench on the old Lutz embankment—that bench invariably occupied by a poor hump-backed woman reading—is sure to be empty at this hour.

It is. We sit down to smoke under the dripping firs, and I go ghost-hunting all alone, in the dark. The memories that are crowded into these few hundred yards! They spring up at my feet, from the damp forest earth. There was once a battle on this site, a sanguinary battle between two rival gypsy bands who used it for their camping ground and accidentally arrived both on the same evening; each claimed it for his own, and several men were killed before the matter was decided; our people were talking about the fray years afterwards. Further on, past the bridge, I murdered the first snake of many and found my first piece of phosphorescent wood. Here, too, stands the rifle-range which is connected with one of six clear memories of my father; he used to come out of the place adorned with paper decorations for his marksmanship and they even hung up a framed diploma of honor to him; the building was sacked two years ago by some local revolutionaries who disapproved of shooting in every form and carried off the diploma, but forgot to efface its mark on the wall where it had hung for fifty years.

Nearly opposite to where we are sitting is a deep incline of grass—I take it to be the bank of the prehistoric Lutz; my father once made me rush up and down this terrific slope in preparation, no doubt, for mountaineering. The quarry close by, in which one hunted vainly for crystals (it is Eocene, and has nothing but spar) is still there, but those mysterious black hillocks by the roadside with their unforgettable smell, where the charcoal-burners plied their trade, are gone and a thriving house and orchard have stepped into their place. The Madonna shrine, further on, is quite unchanged; here the old Anna used to lift me up to gaze at the Mother of God standing, as She does to this day, upon an earth girt about by the green Serpent of Evil. At the back of our bench there used to be a deep, square hole in the ground. My sister and I once informed a newly arrived German governess that it was a disused elephant trap. She said nothing but, on returning home, complained bitterly of our untruthful habits. That plantation of young trees across the road was once a bare, thistle-strewn heath, a *Haide*, the sole locality where, year after year, one could catch white admirals. So there were just two well-known places where you might rely upon a scarlet tiger, and neither more nor less than three, where there was a chance of seeing, though probably not of catching, a *Trauermantel* (Camberwell beauty). Butterflies were dropped, when stones began.

And all this time Mr. R. has had nothing whatever to say. He has grown rather silent of late, his superciliousness begins to evaporate: that augurs well! My theory works—I have observed it for some time past; my theory of the benign influence of woodland scenery upon the character of youth. How much more inspiring to live in such a pastoral and sylvan environment than on the pavements of a town! Instead of troubling about theaters and girls, his mind may well be occupied with some small literary or social problem that befits his age; why Racine went back to antiquity for the subjects of his tragedies, or whether Ronsard really deserves all the praises bestowed upon him. That is as it should be! At last I enquire:

"What have you been dreaming about, this last half hour?"

"Dreaming? Not at all. I have been thinking very seriously."

"What about?"

"What about? About Goethe's 'Hermann and Dorothea.'"

"Ah! I thought so. You are getting on famously. Now, to begin with: where did you become acquainted with that masterpiece?"

"In a French translation, last Christmas. And I was just thinking how true it is, what the mother tells Hermann—when he is in love, you know—you remember?—about the night growing to be the better part of day——"

"Say no more. You are indulging certain thoughts about Tiefis."

"Why not? Perfectly proper ones."

"I might have expected this. Very well. It is a little late to-night, but I suppose we shall have to go there to-morrow. I only hope you share Hermann's exalted sentiments and his purity of heart. Because otherwise, you understand, I could never be an accomplice to such an affair.

ANTS

THAT was a monster of an ant-hill. It was the largest, by far the largest, I ever saw in this country, and the floor of the forest all around was twinkling with these priggish insects. Anxious to have some idea of its true size and anxious, at the same time, not to have any of the nuisances crawling up my own legs, I made Mr. R. pace its circumference. It took him *sixteen* good strides. And there they were, myriads upon myriads of them, hiving up for their own selfish purpose those dried fir-needles which, left alone, would have yielded a rich soil to future generations of men.

I have no use for ants, and cannot regard an ant-heap without yearning to stamp it flat (those made of earth are not difficult to treat in this fashion); without regretting that I lack the tongue and tastes of an anteater. And only in the tropics do you realize what a diabolical pest they may become with their orderly habits; European ants being mere amateurs in obnoxiousness. To do everything you are supposed to do, and nothing else at all; never to make a mistake, or, if you do, to be invariably punished for it in exact proportion to the offense: can there be a more contemptible state of affairs? That is why, even as a boy, I used to foster the independent little fellows called *myrmeleon* (ant-lion) who built their artful, funnel-shaped traps in the dry sand out of reach of showers, just where our house-walls touched the ground; foster them, and visit them periodically, and feed them with these insufferable communists till they were ready to burst. But oh, to be an authentic anteater on a Gargantuan scale—omnipresent, insatiable of appetite— and engulf that entire tribe of automata!

One of my countless grievances against the ant family is that a clever person, long ago, told me that, in order to have the flesh properly removed from the skull of any bird or beast, you have only to lay it in an ant-hill; the insects would do the job to a turn and thank you, into the bargain, for allowing them to do it; work of this kind, he declared, was quite a specialty of their department. Accordingly, I once deposited an extremely valuable relic in the center of a prosperous ant-colony, expecting to find it ready for me, picked clean, after a due lapse of time. On arriving to call for my property, however, a fortnight or so later, I was surprised to find it gone; the methodical socialists had mislaid it, and I never saw it again. One took such losses to heart in those days. I therefore went all the way home once more, determined to get my own job done more conscientiously than theirs, and fetched a rake wherewith this slovenly establishment was leveled to the ground. But oh, for a rake that would rake every ant-hill off the face of the earth!

That happened in my bird-killing period, when I used to get up at the improbable hour of 3:30 a.m. and, putting in my *Rucksack* some bread and smoked bacon-fat and a flask of Kirsch, vanish into the wilds, returning home any time after nightfall or not at all: judge if I saw some ant-hills! So I roved about, and the first thing I ever murdered, an hour after receiving that single-barreled gun, was a melancholy brown owl that blinked at me from its perch below the Bährenloch at Bludenz; the slaughter of this charming bird was taken as a good omen. Soon came other guns, and other birds, not all of which shared the fate of the owl. Never shall I forget a certain pratincole. It was the only one I have yet seen in this province, a great rarity, and it settled down for a whole summer season in the reservoir region along the upper Montiola brook, where it relied upon its disconcerting flight and a trick of rising from the ground at the one and only spot where you could not possibly expect it to do so, to mock all my attempts at bringing it down. I was after it so often that we got to know each other perfectly well, and never bagged it; thereby proving the truth of the local proverb "Every day is hunting day, but not every day is catching day." Queer experiences one had, too. At the age of fourteen I was once resting on my homeward way in the woods near Gasünd, dead tired but uncommonly pleased with myself for having just shot a hazel grouse—again, the only one I ever saw in the province. There came one of those flocks of titmice—is not titmouses the correct English?—accompanied, no doubt, by the inevitable tree-creeper. They amused themselves in the branches overhead and one of them soon struck me as unfamiliar; its size and shape and movements were those of a great tit, but there were unmistakable red feathers on the head and neck. I watched it hopping from twig to twig, annoyed to think that I had shot away my last cartridge, and wondering what this rare mountain bird could be, for I never doubted of its actuality; there it was, before my eyes! Only later did I learn that no such bird exists. Now had the vision been brought about by my state of bodily exhaustion? And was the dream-bird created out of one of those present, or out of nothing at all? Illusion, or hallucination?

Presently certain regions became famous for certain game; in that larch wood between Bürs and Bürserberg, for instance, which takes on such wonderful tints in autumn and which you can enter through a natural arch called the "Kuhloch," you might count on crossbills and on a woodpecker of one kind or another (never on the scarce black one; it haunts the gloomiest forests). Of the lesser spotted species I shot two off the same tree at an interval of almost exactly a year—30 December in one year, and 28 December the next; a circumstance all the more singular, as I never in my life met with another individual of this bird in the whole country. Or, if you wanted a great gray shrike, you had only to go, preferably in winter, to the Scesa-tobel, that devastated tract west of Bürs which was just then beginning to cover itself with vegetation once more. Here you might also put up a hare; it was in the Scesa-tobel, by the purest of accidents, that I once shot a hare in full gallop at a distance of a hundred yards—a mere speck, he was—with a bullet. I confessed afterwards to Mattli, who was beating another part of this torrent, that I had missed him at close quarters with the shot barrel, and soon regretted having made this confession; there are things one might well keep to oneself.

Mattli, whatever his real name may have been, was often with me on such excursions, and I know not how he managed to combine these trips with his official duties as station-master; for station-master he was, at our own station, which was then called Strassenhaus. To be sure, one could take things easier in those days (the building itself was less than half its present size); so easy, that the man who was employed to guard the line a quarter of a mile lower down, used to put up, for several consecutive years, a dummy figure of himself standing upright beside his cabin in the wood, in order to make the night-train people think he was at his post, while he went to booze in a tavern at Ludesch. Yet Mattli's weakness must have been found out in the end; the last time I saw him, he was degraded from his high rank and working in some subordinate capacity at

Bludenz station.

Mattli never felt comfortable unless tracking birds; and his tales of how he shot a great white heron here and a bee-eater there, and something else somewhere else, were enough to make any one's mouth water. He took me in hand, during those lean and hungry years; what the *Brunnenmacher* had done towards fostering my instincts for climbing, Mattli did for the more destructive ones; and a greater contrast was never seen than between these two early mentors of mine. The *Brunnenmacher* was short and fat and bearded and fair-haired and laughing, like many of them hereabouts; Mattli would have struck you at the first glance as something apart from his fellows, something primordial. He towered above the average height, he stooped from sheer tallness; the very scarecrow of a man, dusky, clean-shaven, sallow of complexion, with a harassed and hunted look in his eye and a voice that seemed to come from caverns far away. A lonely, wolfish creature! I never saw him smile. His rarer birds he sold to Mr. Honstetter, the taxidermist of Bregenz, who doubtless disposed of them elsewhere and through whose hands passed nearly every curiosity—lämmergeier, eider duck, cormorant, griffon vulture and what not—which had been obtained in the province or even further afield. He once offered me the skull and horns of a genuine Swiss ibex, and a beaver stuffed by himself which had been killed on the Elbe on the 10 August, 1886; he wanted 175 Swiss francs for this last. The only thing I ever bought there was the skin of an *ibis falcinellus* shot at Hard on the Lake of Constance; it cost me two and a half florins.[16]

---

[16] This particular specimen is commemorated by Rudolph von Tschusi (son of the well-known ornithologist) in "Ornithologisches Jahrbuch," IX, 1898, Heft 2. According to H. Walchner's "Ornithologie des Bodenseebeckens" (1835) the ibis is of the "greatest rarity" on this sheet of water, only a single instance of its occurrence being then known, which is precisely why I bought this one. Apropos of woodpeckers—Bruhin, in his "Wirbelthiere Vorarlbergs" (1868) also says that he saw the lesser spotted kind only once; the bird must therefore be far from common. And this year, for the first time, I had the pleasure of spying the three-toed one. We were walking down from Lagutz to Marul (see p. 155) through that magnificent Alpine forest when we noticed a pair of them. They kept close together, one

Bregenz, however, seldom kept me for more than half a day, since I preferred chasing birds to seeing them stuffed. So I scoured these upper regions over field and forest and rock, covering immeasurable distances and never following a path unless obliged to do so, up to the snow-line and down again, sleeping in hay-huts or remote villages; and judge if I saw some ant-hills by the way; ant-hills in every possible situation; the strangest, after all, being those of dry sand, fetched from God knows where and transported God knows how, and reared-up, Amsterdam-wise, in the middle of watery marshes.

And that particular one, which has led me into this digression—where was it?

Where else, but near Tiefis?

For it stands to reason that we went to that village again, after our nocturnal conversation on the Lutz embankment, in order to visit what Mr. R. calls "the innkeepress and his beautiful girl."

There we sat, all four of us, in that spotlessly clean room, and my companion after consuming his usual horrible mixture—two boiled eggs and a glass of *saft* (a strong kind of cider, of greenish tinge)—straightway opened a fusillade of glances from his flashing black eyes, to which the "baby," so far as I could see, was not insensible.

Her mother, meanwhile, told me what she had heard about the cause of that outbreak of fire which destroyed nearly all the place in 1866. It seems that a party were sitting up one night, as is the custom, beside the dead body of some friend who had expired during the day and, as is also the custom under these mournful circumstances, began to think of refreshing themselves with coffee. There was no milk in the house and it was decided to go into the stable and milk the cow; some straw accidentally took fire from the candle they carried; this started the mischief. Several people were burnt to death on that occasion. A second fire took place in 1868. She said there were

---

following the other and we following both; so tame were they, that we could approach within a few yards and see the yellow on the head of the male. I observed that they had the same habit as the middle-spotted woodpecker, of investigating carefully not only the trunk but the branches of trees. While watching them I thought: how wise of you to have kept out of my way till now!

only two or three of the old houses left; one of them bearing the date 1678——

"What is she talking about?" enquired Mr. R.

"About a fire they had here."

"Can't you two argue outside? And before you go just tell me the German for *embrassez-moi*, will you?"

"How can I tell you, with the mother in the room?"

"Then get her out. Talk to her about wine, in the cellar or somewhere."

"Easier said than done. I think she has intercepted your wireless symbols. They are visible to the naked eye. One could almost catch them in a butterfly net."

"Do you suggest that I was winking, or trying to make eyes?"

"Oh, quite involuntarily."

For one moment, it looked as if his wish were to be gratified. The mother rose from her seat and, opening the door, made as though to enter the kitchen; everything, unfortunately, must have been in order there, for after two paces in the passage she returned to her place beside me once more. That fire—yes! Nowadays, of course, the danger of conflagrations on this scale was growing less and less;[17] the villages were all lighted by electricity, down to the very stables; those inflammable wooden houses, too, were being supplanted by brick or stone, "or the abominable cement," I added——

Meanwhile, that fusillade proceeded without interruption. The "baby" was brightening up under its friendly glow, smiling her innocent smile and sometimes glancing at me as if for confirmation of her pleasure; the mother talked.

"Is the old one never going? Because, for the matter of that, I can do it without saying anything at all; and I will. I would give fifty years of my life.... Just one kiss. I don't want anything more."

"I should hope not. Listen to me for a moment," I went on. "Only a puritan would see any great harm in young people kissing each other, with or without their parents' consent; I feel sure that many happy marriages would never have come about

---

[17] Bludenz itself was twice destroyed by fire. *See* "Vorarlbergische Chronik" (Bregenz, Brentano, 1793, p. 108).

at all but for some such playful preliminaries, and your Dorothea, I must say, looks as if she would not object very violently, provided you did it in a laughing, brotherly fashion. Why should she? Our girls are far too simple-minded to attach that sacramental importance to a kiss which the southern ones do. Observe therefore: I do not pose as a puritan. But please observe also that I am taking for granted that you are serious, both of you, like Hermann and Dorothea; otherwise, of course, I could never be a party——"

"Get her out. Get her out."

"I should like to help you. But you know perfectly well that my acquaintance with the art of outwitting or circumventing parents is of the slightest, and that therefore, quite apart from any moral scruples I might entertain——"

"Get her out."

The "old one" seemed to have taken root. She explained that the fire-brigades, too, were more efficient than they used to be; every village had its own apparatus, and fixed drill on certain days, and fines for those who failed to attend, unless they could show good cause for their absence, such as having to cart their hay in at a moment's notice on account of some threatening thunderstorm——

At last Mr. R. remarked:

"It is all your fault, for making yourself so infernally polite to her. I have often noticed that you cannot leave elderly women alone."

"Excuse me; I make it my business to be civil with everybody, young or old. For the rest, I should be inclined to blame your marconigrams, which are enough to scare any mother. I wonder the poor child is not roasted."

"Roasted! Old men are always cynics."

"Young men are generally fools."

There was that fire at Nüziders as well; how long ago? Fifty years, was it? Perhaps a little more. A tremendous blaze, from all accounts; far worse than Tiefis; and the Fön was blowing so fiercely that sparks were carried right over the Hanging Stone, they said, while people in Ludesch and Thüringen were kept busy all night throwing water on their wooden roofs——

"To oblige me," interposed Mr. R., "just order another quarter liter of wine for yourself. I have thought of something;

it is my last chance. She may have to go downstairs to fetch it. If she does, run after her and say you made a mistake; you want a half. Come back as slowly as possible. Cough, before you enter the door."

The half-liter happened to be on the spot. Decidedly, Mr. R. was having no luck that day. After a very long visit, we bade farewell and walked up past the Bädle inn, Mr. R. complaining grumpily:

"Now what am I to do?"

"Well, you might review the situation, like Hermann did. If I were in your place, I should have no objection to being ultimately connected, by marriage, with the management of a tavern; the position strikes me as offering sundry advantages over the common lot of man. So think it over and, when you have made up your mind for good and all, confide in me and rest assured that I shall be only too delighted to act as interpreter between you and the parents, provided, of course, that your intentions are as honorable as they ought to be."

"Is this the time to make fun of me?"

How sensitive they are, these young people of the guileless variety!

The path we were now following, from the Tiefis "Bädle" to the source of the Montiola brook and thence to the reservoirs, is one of my special favorites. The ground rises slowly, and soon you reach a miniature watershed; whatever drains off behind you flows down westwards and finds its way into the "ruisseau des écrevisses"; the Montiola drops towards the east, at first. Before reaching its source you traverse a wood which Mr. R. immediately christened "la forêt nordique"; he has never seen such a forest save in pictures, yet it certainly recalls them to me, each of the firs resembling its fellow and all at their most uninteresting life-period; this tract must have been cut down and replanted half a century ago, or less.[18]

---

[18] Woodlands have always been cherished here. Wood inspectors were appointed as early as 1626, possibly earlier; they had to traverse the forests every spring, summer and autumn, and to report the slightest damage to the trees. Four years later, an excellent rule was framed to prevent the ever-increasing damage to forest-growth by herds of goats: whoso has three cows, may keep no goat whatever; the owner of two cows may keep one goat; the possession of a single cow entitled you

On issuing from this "forêt nordique" you are already in the Montiola basin, a luscious dank valley surrounded by wooded heights. Presently, on your right, at the foot of the hill, you discern the Montiola fountain. It is an exuberant spring overhung by firs and beeches; almost the entire volume of the streamlet rises at this one point, and you will do well to rest awhile on those mossy stones, as I have done many and many a time, listening to the glad sound of bubbling waters and letting your eye roam across the narrow sunlit vale into the woodlands on its other side. From here the Montiola meanders for half a mile or so, icy cold and full of trout, through a flowery swamp region towards the reservoirs, where it takes its theatrical plunge into the village below.

A distant rocky peak, just to the left of the Hoher Frassen, confronts you on stepping out of the *northern forest*. This is the "Rothe Wand" which, considering its respectable height of 2701 meters, is a decidedly coy mountain, and more clever at hiding itself than most of them; you may obtain another clear view of it from the platform of Frastanz station. It seems incredible that this "Red Wall" which is now climbed by a

---

to three goats and no more. This stamped out the goat mischief. Such were the Lords of Blumenegg, from whom certain modern governments might well take a lesson; like sensible tyrants, they not only laid down wise regulations on this and other matters, but saw to it that they were carried out (those gallows!). In the inhospitable recesses of the Walserthal, at five hours' march from their castle, lying in a caldron of bleak gray crags—an excellent chamois-ground—is the iron-spring and bathing establishment of Rothenbrunnen, where the Alpine rhododendrons droop over your bedroom window; it was the Blumenegg people who erected the first building here in 1650, with accommodation for forty patients. Twenty-six years later they founded a school in the remote hamlet of Sonntag. Their fishery regulations were on the same enlightened scale. As early as 1690 no fishing of any kind was permitted during the spawning season (21 September to 30 November); nets, moreover, were to have meshes wide enough to allow the escape of every fish less than seven inches in length, which happens to be the precise limit fixed, at this present moment, by the conservators of the Exe and other English rivers. For these and other details of the Blumenegg rule *see* the exhaustive monograph on this subject by one of our best local antiquarians, the late Joseph Grabherr, priest of Satteins (Bregenz, 1907).

hundred tourists every year, should in the days of my father have been deemed so inaccessible that he thought it worth while to describe an ascent of it in the transactions of our Alpine Club (1868) in which he speaks of it as "almost unknown." The country has indeed changed since those days, and few pinnacles are left unclimbed; I can mention one of them, at least, for the benefit of anybody who cares to give it a trial. This is the so-called "Wildkirchle" or "Hexenthurm," a fragment of the Kanisfluh *massif* near Mellau, a rock-needle; it has the apparent advantage of being only 140 meters high. All the same, no one has yet stood on its summit, though many have tried to do so; only a couple of weeks ago (23 July, 1922) two young men lost their lives while attempting the feat. My sister, who was the first woman that ever got up the Zimba—and well I remember the state of her leather knickers when she came down again—also had a try at the "Hexenthurm," a little exploit of which I only learnt after her death. She and a guide, from all accounts, were roped together and wound themselves aloft somewhat after the fashion of a nigger climbing a cocoa-palm (I cannot quite visualize the operation); at a certain moment they were only too happy to be able to wind themselves down again.

These were the sports she loved; and I marvel to this hour what made her adopt the married state—she who cared no more for the joys of domesticity than does a tomcat. Talked into it, I fancy, by some stupid relation who ought to have known better.

While strolling homewards from that Montiola fountain hallowed by many memories of my past, I took to relating to my companion all I knew concerning my father's fatal accident, which occurred as he was chamois shooting not far from the Rothe Wand; he fell down a ghastly precipice. Forthwith Mr. R., who has an imaginative and impressionable turn of mind, besought me to take him up there and show him the exact site on the condition, of course, that nothing but English was to be spoken during the trip. Well, why not? No harm in that, no harm whatever; the excursion may distract him, and he has so far seen nothing of these upper Alpine regions. I would gladly go there over the Spuller lake, but cannot bear to see the place again in its changed condition; for this fair sheet of water is now being mauled about by a legion of navvies for the purpose of some miserable railway electrification. Instead of that, we can take the train to Dalaas and mount to the Formarin lake, which lies even nearer to the scene of the accident.[19]

---

[19] During these works at the Spuller lake they unearthed, last year, the skull and horns of an elk; the relic was unfortunately bought by a Swiss who carried it off to his own country; it ought to have gone into the newly founded Bludenz Museum. The Spuller lake is the locality of a strange devil-legend and also of a ghost-story which have been preserved by Dr. F. J. Vonbun in his "Sagen Vorarlbergs" (Innsbruck, 1858). I will transcribe a line or two of the former, omitting his accents and pronounciation marks, in order to give a sample of our Alemannic dialect: "Es set ama wienicht-obed amol en ma zum en andera: 'los nochber, i wetta mi zitgae, du traust di net, mer min schmalzkübelzolfa hinet vo Spullers z holla.' Der nochber set 'woll frile, d wett gilt' und nümt en füfspoeriga hund, stahel, fürste und schwamm und got Spullers zue. Wia-n er an stofel kunnt, bringt em der butz vo Spullers de zolfa a guets stuck scho etgega, aber der nochber set zuenem, los gueta fründ," etc.

GAMSBODEN

THERE is nothing to tell of our walk to the Formarin lake which lies under the precipitous red crags (a kind of marble called *Adneter Kalk*) of the Rothe Wand and thence to the summit of the grass-topped Formaletsch—nothing, save that the Alpine flowers, not so much the rhododendrons[20] as the yellow violets, were a source of considerable interest to my companion. I could have shown him the scarcer Edelraute (*Artemisia mutellina*) which grows on some rocks near the east foot of that hill, but preferred taking no risks and did not so much as mention the plant. Here, also, he was able to inspect a flourishing colony of marmots, a quadruped which, in spite of my assurances to the contrary, he had hitherto been disposed to regard as mythological or imaginary.

I chose the Formaletsch because it is from thence—from its southern base; but Mr. R. rightly insisted on going to the top—that, with the help of a good glass, a distant but clear view can be obtained of the scene of my father's accident while chamois shooting. It occurred, when he was only thirty-six years old, at the Gamsboden heights, so-called from the frequency of chamois to be found there; the place is about a mile off as the crow flies, and on one of its pinnacles you may detect a wooden cross which is perennially renewed by chamois hunters in memory of him; it stands as near to the actual site as most people would care to go. He had just returned from an ascent of the Gross Litzner (or Gross Seehorn)—the second time this peak had ever been climbed (the first was in 1869), and the thing must have happened soon after 7 September, 1874, for that is the date of his last letter to his wife, in which he says: "I shall go shooting for a few days to Spuller and Formarin" (Gamsboden lies midway between these two lakes); "if I delay, I may not be able to traverse any longer the upper grounds, because snow falls there so often and so early." Now hard by that wooden cross is a black precipice which scars the mountain from top to bottom; this is the spot; he fell while

---

[20] The Alpine rose thrives in the climate of Deeside; it grows taller and greener than on these hills, and loses none of its fragrance. It should not be planted in the shade.

attempting to cross the scar, or else, while standing immediately above it on some soil which gave way under his weight; the former is probably the truth. I enquired, but have never heard of any one else essaying the same feat; for my own part, nothing would induce me to proceed more than a couple of yards on that particular surface. For even at our distance of a mile you may guess what it consists of: it is the foul sooty shale called *Algäu-Schiefer*, perfidious and friable stuff, not to be called rock at all save in the geological sense of the word.

Slopes covered by ice or snow have their dangers, so have those decked with the innocent-looking dry grass which, for reasons I cannot explain, is so abhorrent to me that I will make any detour to avoid them; all three of these can be tackled by firm feet and the help of an ax-head as grapnel or for step-cutting. Nothing is to be done, either with feet or with artificial appliances, on an even moderate incline of such Liassic shale, for it yields to pressure and slides down, and this is where a chamois has the advantage over us. A man may scramble about honest crags like a fly on a wall, as securely as any chamois though not so fast; on precipices of the crumbling *Algäu-Schiefer* the animal leaps, and leaps again before the stuff has gathered momentum, and what shall man do? Avoid them, until he has acquired the capacity of bouncing like a chamois; in other words, like an indiarubber ball.

Indeed, shifting material of every kind is objectionable and fraught with peculiar horrors. Up behind Bludenz you may see a row of limestone cliffs called Elser Schröfen, whose foot is defended by a "talus" of rubble which has slowly dropped down from the heights above; and a pretty thing it is, by the way, when you look closely at natural features like this talus, to observe with what flawless accuracy they have been constructed; how these fragments of detritus pass in due order through all gradations of size down the slanting surface, from minute particles like sand at the top to the mighty blocks that form their base. Once, long ago, I conceived the playful project of crossing this rubble-slope from end to end, just below the cliffs. I started on its inclined plane, but had not gone far before realizing the situation. The talus reposed, as it naturally would repose if left to accumulate undisturbed; that is, at the sharpest allowable angle against the cliffs, its upper barrier. It soon struck me as being rather a steep gradient, and not only steep but ominously alive—ready to gallop downhill on a hint from myself; the mere weight of my body could set the whole mass in movement and hurl me along in a rocky flood. While making this sweet reflection I found, with dismay, that it was already too late to turn back; the least additional pressure on one foot might start the mischief; once started, nothing would arrest that deluge; its beginning, without a doubt, was going to be my end.

I was in for a ticklish business. Rush down the slope diagonally and evoke the landslide but anticipate its arrival? Even that was courting disaster. I preferred to remain in the upper regions and there finished the long journey, with curious deliberation, on all fours, in order to distribute my weight; and then only by a miracle. It was one of those occasions on which one has ample leisure to look into the eye of death, and I now wish somebody could have taken a photograph of me—a colored one, by preference; one would like to possess a record of the exact tint of one's complexion during half hours of this kind. Whoso, therefore, intends to traverse the same place would be well-advised to adopt my method of locomotion; the upright posture is not to be recommended. A pleasant farewell to all things! Never a button of you to be seen again; to be caught in a swirl, a deafening cataract of stones and, after snatching *en passant* a few grains of scientific comfort at the thought that your human interference had modified—if only temporarily—the angle of a talus, which is not everybody's affair, to be buried alive at the bottom under an imposing heap of débris.[21]...

---

[21] At the easterly end of these Elser Schröfen there is a convenient path down between the rocks; it connects Marul, via the Els and Furkla alps, with Bludenz. Regarding the cliffs themselves—this decorative ridge seems to be of recent formation; I imagine it is the result of a rupture, and that the hill formerly trended in a soft curve towards the Furkla. When the divulsion took place none can tell; but I think I know where the lost material is to be found, if anybody cares to pick it up. This broken mountain was carried down the Galgen-tobel, and now forms the vast southward-sloping triangle of raised ground which is crossed by the driving-road from Bludenz to Nüziders. On the spot, the existence of a deltoid tract here is naturally not apparent. If you mount to any slight eminence on the other side of the Ill, you cannot fail to

Now boys seem to make a point of doing risky things, whereas a man of my father's age and experience should have made a point of not doing them. What can have induced him to act as he did? He was well acquainted with this particular shale; in that very paper on the Rothe Wand which is the origin of our trip to Formarin, he remarks that the only troublesome part of the ascent was a steep tract of the "soft, crumbling, blackish *Algäu-Schiefer*, which continually slipped away under our feet," adding that "for the rest, no part of the climb could be called dangerous or even difficult." (The present route up there is another and really easy one.) Was it downright bravura? That is not impossible! He had led an enchanted life among the rocks and ice, and a friend of his, an old gentleman whom I saw the other day in Bludenz and who was with him once or twice in the mountains, spoke to me of his contempt of danger; he said that while climbing he "seemed to tread on air" and could not be made to understand what people meant by giddiness. Or was he stalking some particular chamois? In that case the tragedy grows almost intelligible; there are few things a man will not do under those circumstances.

Two others accompanied him on this expedition, Dr. Dürr of Satteins and his own *Jaeger* Fetzel, a native of our village; both have died long since and neither, I believe, was actual eye-witness of what happened at the fatal moment. Many journalistic cuttings and letters relative to this affair, and doubtless giving adequate accounts, were contained in that bundle which disappeared together with other literary and family papers when a certain portmanteau was broken open on its journey; it is a loss I shall never cease to deplore. The ground is supposed to have given way under him; certain it is that he fell from the height, as we were then told, of *many, many church steeples*—a phrase that stuck in my mind; from the height, I should reckon, of some thousand feet. There was nothing about him that was not shattered; his gun, his watch, were broken into

---

perceive its characteristic shape and to divine its origin; it is the work of an agency similar to that which produced the northward sloping delta of the Scesa-tobel immediately opposite. The railway Bludenz-Nüziders skirts at one point a steep grassy bank recalling that described on p. 117; I take it to have been carved into this deposit by the old Ill, in its more vigorous days.

fragments. Strangest of all, even his alpenstock was picked up in several pieces, which gave rise to the conjecture that this implement had betrayed him and snapped under his weight as he leaned on it for support; how else explain the splintering of such light and resilient material? Be that as it may, they carried his remains to Dalaas down the steep and savage Radona-tobel, and anybody who has been there will wonder how they achieved this task.[22] He was laid to rest in the Protestant cemetery of Feldkirch; for the first time in history the bells of all the countryside were tolled at the funeral of a "Lutheran"....

His article on the Rothe Wand is one of several which he contributed to the Journal of our Alpine Club; they can be traced in the files, together with his presidential addresses to the Vorarlberg section, of which I also possess four; one of the most interesting of these papers describes an ascent of the Piz Linard (3416 meters) and Piz Buin and the crossing of the Silvretta and Sagliain glaciers, the latter of which had never been traversed before; it presented *no difficulty*. These writings betray a strong love of nature, and all the exhilaration consequent upon "living dangerously." He was also interested in the scientific aspects of alpinism, as I can see from his marginal annotations to Forbes' "Theory of Glaciers."

More important are two archæological monographs which reveal another facet of his mind; I wish I knew whether he wrote any other such things and where they are to be found; does the library at Bregenz perhaps contain them? The first one (1865, with two diagrams) deals with his excavations on a strangely shaped eminence near Mauren—a village in Liechtenstein, just across our frontier—which he held to be a Celtic hill-fort; his surmise was proved correct by the discovery of certain bronze relics. The other treats of the Roman occupation of this province.[23] It is in the shape of an address to the Museum

---

[22] At the spot where, in later years, the Arlberg railway came to stride over this torrent, a memorial tablet has been erected to him. I was unaware of its existence and only learned the fact two weeks ago— from Baedeker.

[23] Douglass (John Sholto). "Die Römer in Vorarlberg." Thüringen. Im Selbstverlage des Verfassers. 1870. 4to. Paper cover. Title page, two pages index of contents. One page with half title, 67 pages of text. At the end 4 photographic plates, one of them in color.

Society of Bregenz with which he was connected; an exhaustive and conscientiously written memoir, full of ripe speculations of his own, enriched with copious footnotes and citations from those authorities, ancient or modern, who had hitherto touched upon these matters; and defining all remains of antiquity excavated here up to that day (some noteworthy new finds have since been incorporated into the Bregenz Museum). It has given me a feeling difficult to describe, to go through this paper again; I seem to be reading my own lucubrations, for at the same time of life I was writing in the same style on subjects of the same kind; a scholarly digression, for instance, on the Roman roads of the district, *no trace of which exists*, is done quite in my manner of that period. I observe that he contradistinguishes between Celts and Rhætians (p. 6 and note to p. 10);[24] that he

---

[24] He speaks of our primitive lake-dwellers as being of a different race and anterior to these—a race that can be proved none the less to have lingered into the Roman period; which makes him wonder why there is no mention of them in Latin writers, whereas Herodotus has left us such an excellent description. (There is a hint of them in Cæsar's account of the Britons; and a representation, on Trajan's Column, of what might be a Dacian palafitte.) Sundry objects of this epoch have been found at our end of Lake Constance. To other evidence showing that the inner Walgau, the Ill valley between Feldkirch and Bludenz, was at one time also or at least partially a lake, I can add a small confirmatory fact, namely, the discovery by myself, on the 13 October, 1883, of one of those spindle-whorls of burnt clay—unornamented, this one—which are characteristic of the lacustrine era. I drew it out of the earth in the then fresh railway cutting below the convent of St. Peter at Bludenz, and take some little credit to myself for detecting it, and realizing its significance, at that tender age. I know not whether other relics of lake-dwellers have been found up here; this one specimen is sufficient evidence of their existence for me. It is worth noting, too, that not a single old village of the inner Walgau lies in the plain (which may also be due to fear of Ill floods). My contribution to the antiquities of later periods consists of the statuette here figured. It was found not far from Lauterach during those Rhine-regulation works mentioned on p. 54, and I was obliged to give its owner a diamond scarf-pin which had cost me £65—those were opulent days—before he could be induced to part with it. The material is bronze, all except the iron lance-blade and rivetings under the feet; its height, to the tip of the lance, is 17½ centimeters. Every detail in this little work of art is challenging, and I will not lose myself in conjectures as to its age or origin.

---

takes Lindau, and not either of the other two islands, to have been the one occupied by Tiberius; and holds the *Vallis Drusiana*, the Walgau, the heart of our province, to be called not after the Roman general and stepson of Augustus, seeing that the name Druso is of Celtic or Rhætian origin—pre-Roman, in short, and indigenous to this country, whence localities like Drusenfluh, Drusenthor, Druseralp, Druserthal.[25]

Of peculiar interest to me, among my father's writings, are forty or fifty manuscript essays, long and short, on a variety of themes; mere "asides" written, to please himself, in three different languages: English, French and German. French he studied at Geneva; German at the gymnasium of Augsburg, and so successfully, that he learnt to handle that tongue with more freedom and elegance than many a native writer of the country. Most of these miscellanies date from the late fifties or early sixties when he was still young; he doubtless continued to compose them to the end, and the later ones would have a greater value; they are lost. The titles testify to considerable intellectual curiosity: On ambition—The first snowdrop—A woman's thoughts about women—On a passage in Pascal—The carnival—To the memory of ancient Rome—On a comet—Voices of Nature—Friendship—A characteristic of the German language—Dreaming of sounds—On certain pictures in the National Gallery of Scotland—The Lake of Geneva by night—Palleske's Life of Schiller—Suicide—The thunderstorm—Spiritualism—Sunset in autumn—On the want of the habit of

---

[25] Ludwig Steub says that Droussa, Drossa, signifies aldertree or thicket of alders, that the Rhætian form of this word was probably *tarusa* or *trusa*, and that the valley is called *Trusiana* in chronicles, "which may be translated as valley of alders." I have come across it also marked as *Thrusiana*, and may point out that the dwarf mountain alder (*alnus viridis*) is to this day called "Droosle" in our dialect. If Steub be correct, it is an odd circumstance, indeed, that this identical tree should once more have crept into the modern designation of this province: Vor*arl*berg, from the German *Erle*, an elder. "Arlberg"—"Arlenberg" in some old books—has also been derived from "Arla," the dwarf pine, which is said to be one of its names in "German-speaking Rhætia." It may be so. I have never heard these pines called "Aria" hereabouts, though they have several other names (*see* p. 6). They are sometimes called "Adla" in the Bregenxerwald.

writing—The study of Natural Science; and so forth; a

Bronze statue found near Lauterbach

heterogeneous collection! One or two, such as a passionate lament for the death of some little boy-friend, are set in lines as if they were poetry, but there is no poetry about them save a certain rhapsodical elevation of sentiment. Those written in English prove that he had not yet excreted the poison of a German (metaphysical) schooling, which lays fetters upon our thought and dims the candor of literary expression. Immature stuff for the most part, heavy in diction and saturated with the conventional wisdom of youth, although here and there one alights upon something more esoteric, such as (in a "Fragment on Style," 1858): "A noble thought always commands powerful and harmonious expression.... When a truly great thought is clothed in language unworthy of it, the mind which dictated the words can have conceived it only imperfectly"—which strikes me as an unexpected pronouncement, for a youngster of twenty. Altogether, the perusal of these things is a groping, twilight adventure into the soul of a dead man; vainly I ask myself along what lines he would have developed had his life been spared.

Hardly had we reached home again, after a long walk down from Formarin over Lagutz and Marul and Raggal, before Mr. R., who has a sweet nature but is apt to be pig-headed at times beyond the common measure of man, began to complain bitterly that I had shown him no chamois, proceeding thereafter to hint that all my accounts of such animals might well be pure inventions; the chamois-race was doubtless as extinct as the ibex I had shown him at Innsbruck; otherwise, why were they not on the spot, "where they ought to have been," like those marmots? As if the country were a kind of perambulating menagerie! I am all for humoring young people up to a certain reasonable point, but it was a little more than I had bargained for, to start off climbing again that moment. Had he expressed any such wish at Formarin, we might have wandered towards Lech and entered some side-valley on our left, and possibly espied a beast or two among the crags. He said not a word about it up there. And now it was nothing but:

"Show them! Show them! What am I here for?"

"To learn English."

"And to see the sights of the country. Such was our bargain. All you talk about chamois—ah, ah! I begin to understand."

"I showed you a wild roe-deer in the Lutz forest last week, the first you ever saw in your life; and the devil's own job it was to get you to see it. Won't that do?"

"There you made a mistake. You ought to have called it a chamois. Then I should have believed that chamois still exist."

"*Still exist?* Why, we had chamois only the other day for luncheon."

"It might have been bad mutton."

"What next! It was delicious; and no more like mutton than—than——"

"I see what it is. You are afraid of climbing rocks. You have lost your nerve; I noticed it long ago on the cliffs at Scanno, but there are certain subjects one does not like to dwell upon between friends. *Troppo vino.* You comprehend?"

"Nothing of the kind. And if it were *troppo vino*, what object do you gain by being offensive about it?"

"To shame you into showing them."

"Well, after that, I suppose you will have to see them. As to climbing rocks—— I think I can show chamois to people without climbing at all."

So I did; by a stroke of luck which was surely not undeserved. Knowing Mr. R.'s character only too well, and how that there would not be another moment's peace for me until those legendary creatures had been proved to exist, I called to mind, after some little thought, a place where chamois could almost invariably be seen, and we left home then and there, over Bludenz and Brand and the Zalim alp towards the Strassburger hut which lies under the Scesaplana, between a precipice and a perennial snow-field; arriving just as the sun went down.[26] Near the end of our march we turned a little to the right and glanced about us. There they were, three young beasts, almost straight below; unmistakable chamois, and as close at hand as any one could wish. Straightway Mr. R., whose familiarity with precipices is only surpassed by his familiarity with English grammar, proposed scrambling down a sheer wall of several hundred feet, and then throwing stones at them from behind. Who knows? A chance hit on the head, and we might bag one or the other. What a lark, if we did! The novelty of the idea was so alluring that I might have succumbed, if the animals had not scented us—as they would have done ere this, had we been standing below them—and made off amid a resounding clatter of stones. Mr. R. formally declared himself to be satisfied.

"Thank God for that," I replied. "And, now that we are here, I will be able to show you something still funnier and more interesting to-morrow. Butterflies on this snow-field."

---

[26] This last part is the track from which the two young men, referred to on p. 24, contrived to fall and kill themselves. I would take any child up there, though not by night. It may be that they had no nails to their boots and slipped on some rocks freshly glazed with ice, dragging each other over the brink.

"Why not pelicans?"

"Some folks are hard to please."

There are nearly always frozen butterflies to be found up here. They have been wafted from their green meadows into these barren Arctic regions on the upward-striving blasts of the Fön.

Meanwhile we passed the night in the well-heated Strassburger hut, where we discovered as objectionable a crowd of Teutons as I have ever seen gathered together; and I have seen not a few. A fierce argument was proceeding between two of these bullet-headed ones as to whether the snowfield was a *Ferner* or a *Gletscher*. The *Ferner* man was right (though the Tyrolese use the word "Fern" for a glacier); but his opponent also came in for some share of applause. He had the louder voice of the two.

Up the Scesaplana next morning in time for the sunrise, where Mr. R. grew silent and respectful. Naturally enough. For there is something oppressive to the spirit on being thus islanded, for the first time, in a glittering ocean of Alpine peaks, and breathing the icy air of dawn at 3000 meters. I greeted old friends that arose up round us, and my glance, turning eastwards, rested at last upon the stainless white dome of the Ortler, fifty or sixty miles away. I called to mind that short snow-arête just before you reach the summit, knife-like and not even level; would I now care to run along it as I did then? Well, that was in the eighties and perhaps they have built a railway up the Ortler by this time; in the eighties, while we were touring on old-fashioned high bicycles over the Stelvio pass—a record, I fancy: there was a notice of it in the C. T. C. Gazette; over the Stelvio into Italy and back by the Splügen, riding home in one day from the Post at Splügen over Thusis and Chur and Ragatz and Feldkirch—which was also something of an achievement for the wretched machines of those days.

On the way down we stepped for a moment into the Lünersee hut, where Mr. R. had a look at the large photograph of my father after whom the place had been named, then followed the Rellsthal towards Vandans under that formidable flank of the Zimba on which the other tourist had died of sheer fright. During this descent my companion, unfortunately, began to relapse into something like his normal frame of mind; that is to say, our pleasure was nearly marred by persistent jocular allusions to that London hat of mine which has not yet ceased to provoke his merriment. Some time ago I was under the impression that he had forgotten this trivial and well worn theme of mirth. Far from it. Young people never will realize when a joke has grown threadbare, and he now distilled so much fresh laughter out of its shape, its color, its brim and other details of construction, its general fit, its suitability to my particular style, likening me at one time to his own countryman Napoleon and at another to a certain old female cousin of whose existence I had hitherto been unaware, that I was on the verge of getting annoyed when I hit upon the genial expedient of making him translate his miserable witticisms into the English tongue.

Then, and not till then, did they become really amusing; it was my turn to laugh.

JORDAN CASTLE

WE often walk past that decrepit castle of Jordan. Situated on the hill above Bludesch, it is a landmark visible from afar, and was never a castle at all but a pretentious kind of villa. My mother told me that the builder had been a Dutch political refugee, and that the red violets growing on the inside of its westerly wall were planted by him. Those violets may be found to this hour—their leaves, at least; and you may find white ones along the path that leads down eastwards out of the orchard here—you could, at least.

Since then I have learnt a little more, but not nearly enough, about this strange-looking ruin. There used to be a small, two-roomed house on the site in olden days; this was bought, and converted into a splendid palace—*splendidum exstruxit palatium*—by Georg Ludwig von Lindenspeur, who lived there till his death in 1673. The plan of the building is as regular as can be, and thoroughly uninteresting; it has an artificial terrace in front, supported on massive substructures. The place continued to remain in good state till 1843 when it changed hands, and the new proprietor, having no use for it, took off the roof and carried away everything else that served his purposes. Who Lindenspeur was, I cannot say; the name does not sound altogether German or Austrian, and is unknown to me. He it was, I imagine, who for his own convenience or that of his visitors built or enlarged the path that leads up, some few hundred yards to the east of the ruin, from the driving-road in the valley below; this path, then broad enough for a carriage, with sustaining walls on both sides, has now grown quite narrow from disuse. He also founded a charity for several villages which exists to this day. The yearly income, for our particular one, is twenty-two florins; before the war, one might have helped a few poor people with this sum. Who is going to pick it up nowadays?

Such is the history of the "Jordanschloss." I should like to learn more about the mysterious Lindenspeur; where he came from, and what induced him to settle in these outlandish regions and there to live to the day of his death. I have heard of no one else doing such a thing in the seventeenth century. He may well have been a refugee of some kind; a recluse, an original, in any case, and a wealthy one. So Jordan has been a ruin only for the last eighty years. One would never think so; for it already wears a hopelessly decayed look, as if it had been abandoned for a couple of centuries at least. That is because it lacks the solid masonry of our feudal remains. It crumbles away all the time, and I suspect that the farmhouse near at hand has been built with its stones.

We had a good look at Jordan yesterday afternoon, and agreed that it was an uncommonly transparent fabric. "The old gentleman must have been fond of windows," observed Mr. R. True! There are more open spaces than stones in its ostentatious front; a row of eleven windows, all exactly alike, and young trees are sprouting out of them. This is what made Mr. R. christen the place "Château aux fenêtres." And this name, in its turn, gave occasion for a simple question on my part, a question that led to a prolonged and painful discussion, in the course of which some little light was thrown on Mr. R.'s progress in the English language. I enquired as I should have done:

D. Now what is the English for "Le château aux fenêtres"?

R. The castle to the windows.

D. Castle to the windows? Try again. I am the most patient teacher in the world. And we have the whole afternoon before us. So don't hurry and don't disappoint me. Think!

R. Let me see.... "Château" may sometimes be rendered by "country-house." The country-house to the windows. I know my *vocables*.

D. Your stock of words will pass; and such praise as is due to you for having gotten them by heart should not be withheld. But you will never learn English. "Castle to the windows" is treating our language in your usual brigandish fashion; *de haut en bas*. How often have I told you that a language must be courted, like a lover!

R. Never learn English? Are you serious? If so, allow me to say that I have already learnt more than enough to pass my examination. I know my *vocables*, as you yourself admit. I am also acquiring a little more polish, which I confess may still be needful. And latterly—how I have learnt to converse!

D. Yes; how! This is most discouraging, after all my efforts. Castle to the windows—good God! It might drive a less optimistic tutor crazy. Let us sit down on this stone for a moment, and I will tell you something that has just occurred to me. There was once a Greek poet and grammarian called Palladas, who was favored, like myself, with promising pupils of your style; who was a teacher, I mean, and nearly committed suicide in consequence——

R. They never do it, those fellows, although one wishes they would. It is the pupils who sometimes kill themselves. Your Pylades is probably alive to this day. Well?

D. Well, during one of his fits of depression at their extraordinary intelligence, he wrote a little couplet which still exists to prove the depth of his despair. Believe me, I can sympathize just now with the unhappy Palladas. The castle to the windows.... Would you like to translate his two short lines? They are very easy. And then you will understand the state of my feelings.

R. Not if you write in Greek. Put them into French, and I will translate anything you please. Here is a scrap of paper.

D. ...There now! Go ahead. No, no, no. I must have it in writing. You are too slippery, *viva voce*. And please try to do it carefully, for a change.

R. Voilà!... *I was ramble nude to the earth, and I will ramble nude underneath her. And why I dredge in vain, viewing the nude finish?* So that is the state of your feelings. You seem to have forgotten to put your clothes on.

D. I was ramble nude——

R. You may say "stroll" instead of "ramble"; I am not particular! Or "saunter." All these are better words than "walk" or "promenade"; they are more adapted for poetic uses. That is why I chose "dredge" instead of "labor"; it sounds less common. You see what come of knowing one's *vocables*.

D. Drudge; not dredge. I was ramble nude. This is appalling. I mean to preserve that document as a *pièce justificative*. There may be some trouble, you know, about the way you have spent your time out here. Ramble nude—God Almighty! Why, the poet means to say that he walked, that he was born, naked into this world; don't you see?

R. n*Ça se peut bien.* In that case, he was perhaps not the first. There is nothing very original in baby-poets being born naked. Now if he had worn a felt hat on that occasion——

D. This is hardly the moment, is it? Your English, I must

insist on telling you, leaves a great deal to be desired. And I should like to ask: what are we going to do about it?

R. If the baby-poet had suddenly come to light, wearing that London hat of yours ... ah, the doctor's explanations———!

D. Laugh away. There will be a nude finish. You will never pass the test.

R. And why not? Only a camel would bother to learn all those useless idioms. I was always first in our English class at college. I knew more than the *profs*, and they were high-class people.

D. Was you ramble nude there?

R. Allons; just a little more polish ... ah, ah! The horrified *sage-femme* ... her face ... ah, ah, ah!...

From this transparent "castle to the windows" we "rambled" yesterday, always to the westwards, always along the brow of the hill; crossed the Tiefis-Bludesch road and, about a quarter of a mile further on, turned to the right and followed a field path that goes first uphill and then down. It leads to the village of Schlins.[27]

The meadow region ends in a dank spot, almost a swamp, surrounded by forest on three sides. We were amazed at the multitude of butterflies crowded into this narrow space: I have never seen so many swallowtails gathered together. The mead is henceforward to be known as "pré des papillons," and it was here that Mr. R. propounded a puzzling question. What happens to all the butterflies, he asked, when the grass is cut and the

---

[27] Nothing is known, I fancy, of the meaning of those old place-names like Schlins, Düns, Röns, and so forth. The origin of our Thüringen is held to be different from that of the German province, which has been derived from Turo, a family name; to be Celtic, and allied to Tours and Zürich (which is also marked as Türrig in old maps); to this day our people invariably call the place "z'Türrig." Schlins is the birthplace of a remarkable man, Magister Bartholomæus Bernhardt, born 1487. He was called Velcurio from the neighboring town of Feldkirch, studied (1504) at the new University of Wittenberg which within twenty years had received over forty students from Vorarlberg; became a monk and (1519) rector of that University; thereafter to the end of his life Prior of Kemberg in Saxony. According to Sebastian Münster (1550) he was the first priest to take to himself a legitimate wife. He died 1551. His brother John, who seems to have been also a monk, wrote a commentary on Aristotle's "Physics" and was likewise married.

flowers gone? Where do they go? What do they find to eat? I have no idea. There are butterflies everywhere just now. In a fortnight or so, there will be none left, save a few peacocks and red admirals moping about the fallen fruit in orchards. Have they migrated upwards into Alpine quarters, where the fields are mown at a later season? Do they perish?

Here, at the end of the "pré des papillons," you enter a noble forest which continues as far as Schlins. We used to call it the wood of the——. No; I refuse to open up that chapter of infantile nature-worship. Suffice to say, that the forest was properly dedicated to this potent but capricious deity, both by reason of its immeasurable distance from home (nearly an hour's walk) and consequent unfamiliarity to us, and of the deep gloom which pervaded it in those days. It has since been thinned out; even to-day it remains one of the finest in the district and many of the firs reach a height of forty meters. Lower down and to the south there runs through the same wood another path, also to Schlins. It follows the base of one of those waterless east-west vales which are so contrarious, because, instead of at right angles, they lie parallel to our main valley. This used to be a terrifying track in those days; so narrow and deep was the dell, so tall and thick the trees on either side, that twilight reigned here in bluest noonday; and its length was interminable! The whole glen has now been reafforested and sunshine penetrates into all its recesses; but you can still discover the decaying stumps of those old giants, encrusted, many of them, with *Elfenbecher* (fairy goblets)—minute mossy growths, shaped and tinted like chalices of frosted silver.

As we traversed this lovely wood of the——, we were startled by a disquieting din on our right. It was only a frolicsome shower, pattering deliciously among the beeches yonder. Soon it reached us and drove us under a fir. Here, as the drops were trickling through the branches, my companion drew from his pocket that talisman, that *vade mecum* and *sine qua non*, and performed a selection of pieces grave and gay; I went to inspect a small cross that stood close at hand—one of four which are erected in this forest to the memory of woodcutters who have perished at their trade. It is dated 1867 and records that the victim was 63 years old. There is another, bearing a naturalistic representation of the accident; a wife on her knees, the husband lying dead beside her, with a massive log of timber stretched across his middle.

Now the loud rain dropped suddenly to a whisper and we went forth again towards Schlins, inhaling the aromatic odors of those essential oils which it had wakened out of the damp ground. The way is marked by colored signs against the trees; they have not been renewed since the war, and are fast fading away. This is a relic of the activities of the Blumenegg "beautification-society" which was started in emulation of that of Bludenz and, like it, expired in consequence of the war. The society did a good deal in its short life in thus marking tracks and even building benches here and there, that now molder pleasantly away; the whole wood from St. Anne church to Nenzing, for instance, is provided with marks, and whoever does not know the country might well be grateful for them. They also built the road down to Blumenegg waterfall, a delightful spot; that along our big waterfall was made by my brother and inaugurated, amid much speechifying and beer-drinking, on the 31 July, 1898.

Schlins lies prettily tucked away on a green level between the hills and the projecting woodland ridge of Jadgberg. We soon found ourselves at the Krone inn, where I have been an habitué for more years than I care to remember and where Mr. R. devoured his customary two eggs and cider, while I indulged in a long chat with the proprietress, who is a particular friend of mine. It does one good to be with such people, so blithe and natural and intelligent; I could go on talking to her for ever and ever; and I nearly did.

Then up, at last, through the firs to the venerable ruin of Jagdberg. Hard by the castle they have erected the so-called "Josefinum"—a kind of refuge and school for poor children of both sexes, waifs and strays, the scum of the province. It contains about fifteen girls and fifty boys, many of questionable parentage or none at all, ailing in body and mind—squint-eyed and one-legged and tuberculous and mangy and feeble-minded and depraved. They are sometimes spoken of as the "Verbrecherle," the little criminals, and a few may perhaps deserve that name. One of these, not long ago, certainly displayed a rare tenacity of purpose. It was a boy-orphan who, at the age of fourteen, left the establishment where (according to his own account) he had been grossly and systematically ill-treated. When he was eighteen he considered himself strong enough to carry out a long-meditated project of revenge, and stole into the place one night with the intention of setting fire to it and of murdering the director with a dagger or revolver, both of which he carried on his person. They caught him before much damage could be done, and he was sentenced to eight years' imprisonment. The son of a gypsy, it was said; which may be an *ex post facto* explanation of his original conduct. In every case, he cannot but have suffered under an oppressive sense of injustice to be able to nurse his rage through four long years. Perhaps, after serving his sentence, he will have another try at the director....

As at Blumenegg, there is nothing left of Jagdberg save its outer wall, its shell; and on entering this hoary shell we were amazed to find therein a modern swimming-bath of cement, surely the most unexpected use to which a feudal ruin can be put. A handful of boys were splashing about here, together with some school-children from Schlins, every one of whom is obliged to learn to swim. This bath and the Josefinum and its plantations have impaired the charm of Jagdberg, as I knew it long ago; it was then a slumberous, world-forgotten place. I am glad they have at least not troubled to tear down its magnificent growth of ivy. True, it always lacked the seclusion and dreaminess of Blumenegg; on the other hand, it is more spacious, more solid, more grandiose. Like that ruin, it dates from about the twelfth century, was destroyed by the Appenzellers in 1405, and afterwards rebuilt; within its walls stood a famous chapel dedicated to St. Michael. It must now have lain abandoned for many long centuries. One would like to know why Herr Georg Ludwig von Lindenspeur, who seems to have had more money than was good for him—why he did not settle down in this wonderful place, instead of erecting his flimsy and pompous barrack at Jordan? Who would not live at Jagdberg, if he could? Such thoughts occur involuntarily, on visiting any of these old sites. Who would not live at Jagdberg, especially in that earlier period? Then down with that warren of rickety and vicious bastards, and up with the gallows!

Charitable projects....

And yet——

And yet these lords of Jagdberg and other men of the past may not have been altogether the simpletons one used to think them. When they risked their lives, they did it in their own interests and on their own responsibility; not, like our warriors of to-day, for the sake of enriching people of whom they had never even heard. When they robbed, they robbed to some purpose that was at least seemingly sane and seemingly profitable. They had not much use for the brotherhood of all men: "God save us from such brothers!" we can hear them saying. And so much one may observe without bitterness, that if one dream can be called more absurd than another, this of universal brotherhood is surely the absurdest that ever sat in our poor deluded brain, and the present state of the world a luminous commentary on it. I imagine it would have puzzled those old feudals—our Oriental preoccupation with other folk, our craving to lean up against each other for mutual support and betterment. Flabbiness, they might have called it. We call it "solidarity."... A little trick of ours.... We invent such words to shadow forth a desire more or less vague, more or less reasonable; and forthwith flatter ourselves that we have succeeded in creating a thing. Solidarity! Mankind is a jellyfish. How comes a jellyfish to want a backbone?

Such individualistic ideals may come into fashion again. Meanwhile, they are out of date. The castles lie in ruins and their occupants, the human wolves, have been hunted out of the land. Let us be sheep. The loves and hatreds of these wolfish creatures must have been narrow and limited in their range. On the other hand, they were doubtless personal, fervent. They were kept clean. Our loves and hatreds are no longer kept clean. They have ceased to be personal; we love and hate in the herd, the mass. Endeavoring to identify our most intimate aspirations with those of other men, we produce that incongruity of feeling and outlook, that haziness of moral contour, which is a feature of modern life—to what end? Solidarity! By all means adopt a fellow-creature's greatcoat, or lend him your own. Why adopt his character? Is a bundle of self-contradictory inhibitions worth adopting? Love your neighbor as yourself. Now what has that gentleman done, to deserve our love?

Philanthropic musings, engendered by the spectacle of Jagdberg and its Josefinum....[28]

---

[28] This reads a little jaundiced. I must contemplate my oleographs.

ROSENEGG

ANOTHER of these castle-ruins is the massive old tower of Rosenegg near Bürs (Rhæto-Roman *Puire*), opposite Bludenz. It also dates from the twelfth century; like the others, it was sacked by the Appenzellers in 1405; unlike them, it was never rebuilt—not till the other day. For six long centuries it stood desolate and forlorn. Then, quite lately, somebody bought the place and converted it into a residence; with good taste, so far as one can judge from the outside. All the same, it is annoying to see that he has planted a few exotic conifers in the grounds; they will doubtless prosper there, but they are out of harmony with their Alpine surroundings. I must come and pull them out, one of these nights.

The Rosenegg I knew was a truly "somber pile," decaying alone up there, far from the habitations of men, on its sunless hillock under the shadow of those mighty Rhætian peaks. Nobody ever seemed to go near the place. There was a shattered window at a good height on the eastern flank, and you could get in here by climbing a wild cherry tree and then jumping on to its ledge. The interior was a moldering chaos of stones. Round about we used to find certain favorite plants: the rose-and-white immortelles with silvery leaves, and "fox-tail" moss, and the globular amber-hued ranunculus of spring, deliciously fragrant. Then flowers were dropped in favor of butterflies; after that, the stone-period began and Rosenegg was again frequented, for the whole neighborhood happened to be strewn with crystalline erratics great and small, and in some of them you might find brown garnets, but not in all; far from it! You had to look for them pretty closely.

That was long ago.

And now, at the other end of life, one returns anew to Rosenegg on a sunny afternoon, purged of the mists of middle years and, delving into memories of that clear dawn and seeking to recapture its spirit, marvels at the feverish joy which greeted discoveries such as these degenerate little garnets, not a single one of which had the right color, nor made the faintest pretense at being the rhombic dodecahedron it should have been. How one changes!

This was always, alas, a bad country for "stones."... Silver ore near Dalaas of questionable worth, and rock crystals in several quarries, and gypsum beyond St. Anton, and a poor kind of amethyst at the Hanging Stone; the fossils were likewise meager—corals in the limestone of Lorüns, univalves under certain rocks at Hohenems, those oysters in the ruddy Nagelfluh (Middle Miocene) at Bregenz; last, not least, the fucoids of the Flysch (Eocene) which you could find nearly everywhere, pretty to look at, but terribly fragile. That was all. There were legends, mere legends, of ammonites being seen in the local red marble; we never saw them![29] Ah, if our father had still been alive, he might have told us where to find this or that; his stone-collection was our delight, our despair. Not everybody had his luck, we often said, to stumble in the Scesa-torrent upon a huge writhing mammoth tusk that required two or three men to carry—how had he done it, and why couldn't we do it too?[30]

Stones were dropped when birds and beasts began, and during that slaughter-epoch Rosenegg became once more famous for producing the first stoat that ever fell to my gun, and a falcon as well. There was a pair of them here, and once, resting on that green terrace with my mother, I saw the male bird dash off the ruin overhead, and swiftly took aim at him (I refused to be parted from my gun, even during family walks). Down he fluttered and fell, stone dead, at our feet. I recall that afternoon as if it were yesterday. My mother said nothing; she suffered more intensely than did the falcon, but had long since abandoned all hope of curing my murderous instincts. I remember, too, passing alone once through the woods below this tower and becoming aware of an unusual sound at my side. Who could have guessed its origin? It was a putrid fragment of a stag, so alive with worms as to make itself heard.

At the back of Rosenegg a little path descends through the wood; here, one morning before sunrise, I came face to face with a fox who was returning from some nocturnal visit to the poultry yards of Bürs; it was a question of who should step aside

---

[29] They do not exist in this *Adneter Kalk.* We noticed some fair specimens the other day at the Freiburger Hut (Formarin).

[30] This tusk has been in the Bregenz Museum since 1859, with a suitable inscription. A molar, presumably of the same animal, was found by a peasant in this torrent some twenty years ago; it is now at Invery House, Banchory, N. B.

to let the other pass. The fox was not to be outdone in politeness; he vanished ere I had time to slip the gun from my shoulder. This is the path we followed yesterday, proceeding thence always eastwards at the foot of the Rhætikon mountains; at their roots, one might say, for they rise up straight from the level, as does a tree. Walking along, Mr. R. encountered a tiny creature that scared him considerably; indeed, he was transfixed with astonishment and stepped a pace or two backwards; he had never yet seen anything of the kind, either on land or in water.

"A crocodile?"

"Not quite; a Quadertatsch. Pick him up and make friends with him."

"His hands are cold."

Cold they are, like those of a Hindu; and he himself is blacker than any Hindu, or any nigger; black as the devil, with a luster as of patent-leather boots; black but comely. It looks as if his first shape had been remodeled by some thoughtful craftsman who added a row of decorative bosses along sides and back, and pinched his tail till it became slightly quadrangular in form; creating, with these few masterly touches, something heraldic and distinguished out of quite a commonplace original. A vast improvement! And his manners are in keeping. He nods his head sagely on making your acquaintance, and at once begins climbing up your arm with a comical precision of movement, a deliberate jauntiness, that reminds one of some retired *maître de ballet* whose limbs have grown a little creaky with age and rheumatism, but who is determined to show off his faded graces to the best advantage.

Perhaps I ought to explain that the Quadertatsch is what the Tyrolese call a Tattermandl. The last syllable of this word proves that they have also noticed certain human traits in his demeanor. The Tattermandl is a universal favorite among Alpine folk. In his home up there, you seldom see one of them alone; they are social beings, often to be found in companies of a dozen or more. And what was this one doing here, all by himself? Like several others I have met, he has been the victim of an accident; always the same accident! He was swept off his legs in the recent torrential rains and whirled two or three thousand feet down, into our tropical regions, along one of the gullies that seam these mountains. He will have a long walk home again; and all uphill.[31]

Two hours later we had crossed the Ill at Lorüns and found ourselves, after a good while, walking up the picturesque village of Rungalin; it leans against the hillside near Bludenz in the shape of the letter Y, and should be viewed in spring, when its brown houses are all smothered in creamy apple blossoms. Thence, always uphill, past the little spring called "Halde Wässerle" and along the summit of those fine cliffs at whose foot lies the Bährenloch cavern, turning sharp to the right and emerging finally at Obdorf, beside the upper bridge that spans the Galgen-tobel.

Just across this torrent, where the path begins to climb to Latz, stands a modern peasant house which I never fail to visit with pleasure and even respect. It has a suggestive history. Years ago, there was a poor man who went, with all his family, as a dayworker to the cotton-mill at Bürs, and there earned what he could. Such people are everlastingly in want, since for some reason or other all their gains have to be spent forthwith; this particular family was no exception. The father watched his children growing thinner and paler from day to day, and stupider and wastefuller in character, and saw no prospect of any betterment in the future. "This must end," he suddenly said, as if an inspiration had come to him; and, borrowing a little money, bought for next to nothing the tract of ground here which was then almost a marsh (nobody would believe, nowadays, that you could pick handfuls of the large single gentian on the spot), and drained it, and built a small cottage. The family became agriculturists then and there; not a single member returned to the factory, not for a day. Every year something new was done to their domain; a cow purchased, another strip of land bought, a fresh room added, and so on; with the result that these people, instead of empty heads and

---

[31] "Mounts up to 7000 feet, and probably descends not much below 3000," says Schreiber, in his *Herpetologia Europea*. Bludenz lies at half the latter elevation. Brehm draws the word Tattermandl from "toter Mann," which is a philologer's derivation; he is anything but "tot." It might be a corruption by popular etymology, of the Latin and Italian name. Bruhin says that *salamandra maculosa* occurs at Thüringen. I have traversed every inch of the Thüringen territory in all seasons and weathers for the last half century, and never seen one.

spendthrift habits and weakened constitutions, have now acquired prosperity and self-respect and decent manners and good health. Here was one, at least, who refused to be beguiled by the tomfoolery of industrialism.

We descended to Nüziders down the gentle slope of that deltoid tract mentioned on p. 148. It had grown late, and my companion was proportionately hungry after his long walk; he insisted on refreshing himself at the "Bädle" inn which in olden days used to be an excellent tavern run by a Swiss—as children, we were once quarantined within its walls for a week or two, to escape an epidemic of measles, and all in vain! Immediately overhead are the ruins of Sonnenberg castle, another of our feudal nests and not the least famous of them; to judge by prints, it must have been a lordly structure. It was destroyed by fire, and nothing remains upright save a wall with a couple of trees growing out of its masonry. The last survivor of this noble family ended in ignoble fashion; he was murdered by another count whom he had enraged with some saucy speech.

It was dark and moonless night before Mr. R. could be brought to confess that he had eaten enough for the time being; none the less, we risked taking the uphill path which starts at the "Bädle" and traverses the wooded saddle behind the Hanging Stone, to end near the church of St. Martin on the other side of that ridge. The now defunct "beautification-society" of Bludenz did much to improve tracks like this and those we had followed earlier in the afternoon; their labors were then lost on us, everything was pitch black before our eyes; there was no break whatever in the forest, and a man might well go astray here at a late hour, particularly at a certain point where, instead of turning to the left, he would be tempted to go straight on, and presently find himself on the edge of a nasty cliff. The place, however, was still familiar to me, since it was up here that I used to lie in wait with the saturnine Mattli, at nightfall ages ago, trying to poach roe-deer. I can still hear him whispering to me, on such an occasion, in that sepulchral voice of his:

"You know what happened there?"

"Where?"

"Down in that hollow," and he pointed with his gun in the direction of a sunken patch, a dingle, at our feet; it lies in the center of the saddle.

"What happened?"

"They killed the last wolf."

"Oh!"—and I felt a little shudder running down my back.[32]

I was thinking yesterday of Mattli and his last wolf, as we moved forward through the night, and thereupon began to puzzle over a question which seems to have puzzled no one else, namely, how it comes about that this animal is extinct in all the Alpine region, notwithstanding its enormous area of inaccessible territory, whereas in relatively populous districts such as the Dordogne it is still common enough to be something of a nuisance, in spite of ceaseless persecution on the part of man. I concluded, perhaps wrongly, that the wolf has been extirpated hereabouts not so much by the human race as by hunger; his natural prey (hares, wildfowl, etc.) having grown much scarcer of late—scarcer than they are in Scandinavia or Russia, while sheep and goats and dogs, which he can still pick up in places like the Vosges or Apennines, are not so easy to capture during the severe alpine winter, being mostly kept within doors. If he could go to sleep like the bear, or had the cunning of the fox, he might have survived to this day.

At last we emerged on the level again and, passing the church of St. Martin, found ourselves under the lights of

---

[32] Mattli was right. According to Bruhin's "Wirbelthiere Vorarlbergs" (1868) the last wolf was shot at the Hanging Stone about 1830, though he does not mention this fact in his interesting paper on the fauna and flora of this cliff. The last lynx, he says, was killed about 1820; a certain Rüf, a well-known chamois hunter of the Bregenzerwald, told me that when he was a youngster he frequently came across old Lynx-traps in the woods. There are woodcuts both of lynx and wolf in Schlee's "Rhetia"; he speaks of them as being very troublesome in the Bludenz district (p. 61). The wild boar, long since extinct, he mentions among the game animals of Bregenz and Dornbirn. I myself found the tusk of one during some drainage works in the fields between Bludenz and Rungalin. Bruhin says that a bear was killed near Nenzing in 1828 and that another one frequented an alp there for a whole summer season in 1867. Bears were passably common when Tschudi wrote his "Thierleben der Alpenwelt"; Berlepsch (about 1860) says that twelve to twenty of them were still annually killed in the Alps; soon enough, I shall be one of the few persons left who have tasted the flesh of a genuine Alpine bear. This was at Nauders in the Tyrol in May, 1897; the beast had probably come over from the Grisons.

Ludesch. Never before had that village seemed so endlessly long.

Those gray, weather-beaten erratics of which I spoke have been gradually disappearing from the landscape since my Rosenegg days. They used to be quite a feature of the countryside. When you crossed our petrifying stream, for instance, you beheld a horde of them scattered over the slanting field below the road, and some were of prodigious size, bearing bushes and little trees on their backs. Not one of those is left; I know of only a single remaining block which is decorated with timber; you will never find it, though you may certainly pass a spot, not far from Jordan castle, where twenty-three can still be counted lying about—dwarfs, mostly, or half submerged in the earth. The peasant makes war on these things; he shatters them in pieces with dynamite or splits them with wedges; for they take up room, they interfere with his mowing operations, their stone is admirably adapted for building purposes. And here is another little puzzle. Sometimes, in a thick wood, one may stumble upon the conscientiously piled-up fragments of what used to be a block of this kind, all forgotten and overgrown with moss; why go to the trouble of breaking up this fractious material, and then do nothing with it? Mystery!

The wall of the road leading up from the Bludesch church of St. Nicholas towards Tiefis consists largely of the primitive rock of erratics which formerly strewed the surrounding land; so does that which leaves Tiefis in the direction of our own village.

Which reminds me of our last, and most disappointing, visit to the "innkeepress and his beautiful girl." There was no question, that day, of the *embrassez-moi* on which Mr. R. has set his simple heart, for the baby was absent, having gone for a brief "Sommerfrische"—as if Tiefis were not fresh enough already—up to Thüringerberg, to stay with a sister of her mother's, who comes from there. She would be back in a few days, we were told. A piece of downright bad luck for him! He seemed to be really upset; so much so, that I had to promise we should return again soon. Then he suddenly recalled my undertaking to show him over the Valduna asylum; it would be an agreeable diversion and fill up the time; we could run down to Bregenz too, as he had never seen a great inland water like the Lake of Constance.

My passion for idiots having waned of late, I was hoping he had forgotten about Valduna. But no. He may forget the past participle of every one of our irregular verbs; the prospect of an exhibition of three or four dozen lunatics is the kind of thing he can be trusted to remember. So be it. After all, there is no harm in going there; no harm whatever. The sight of those poor wretches may medicine his youthful bumptiousness and make him more contented with his own lot in life which, once a week or so, gives occasion for some ludicrously savage outburst.

VALDUNA

VALDUNA was a surfeit of idiots. Mr. R. waxed grave; he has gained, I think, a definite acquisition of humanity. That is as it should be. Such sights of anguish are a tonic for the soul; they make us serious about things that are worth being serious about; they deepen and broaden our sympathies.

The cheery doctor became still more cheery on hearing my name—he is a local alpinist—and did not omit a single patient save one or two of the women who, presumably, were taking sun-baths in *impuris naturalibus*, as was also one of the males, a robust and pretty boy of sixteen; he had a clouded, far-away look, and could not be induced to utter a word. We saw them all; the unclean patients, the unquiet patients, as well as the simple lunatics, sad or glad. There are no violent ones here just now, but some of those who suffered from hallucinations of hearing were sufficiently abusive.

"Hello, Madam," said the doctor to one of the ladies, "what may you be doing here? I don't seem to have seen your face before. "

"I've come to visit a poor patient. Didn't they announce my name? How unpardonably stupid of them! But I shall have to be leaving in about half an hour. So good-by, doctor, in case we don't meet again."

Quite mad!

There was a poor old fellow in bed, on the brink of G. P. I. He fascinated Mr. R., casting a hot, delirious glance upon him and pouring out a flood of turbid megalomania.

"What is he telling me? What? What's that? Translate, translate!"

Translating was out of the question. The speech contained not a shred of coherence; nothing but fragmentary pictures, flashing up and swiftly engulfed again; his brain was in combustion. Moreover, the patient would have had ten words out of his mouth to every one of mine.

We visited the other establishment as well, a non-official, charitable one. The director is a priest, native of this province, and one who knows it well. He told me an interesting thing. We were speaking of the former wine-production here, and I said it was doubtless the Arlberg tunnel (I went through with the first train) which had caused the local plantation of vineyards to cease, or at least to diminish to such an extent that, for example, of the vineyards once clothing the hillsides of my particular village—our family, too, had its own—there was only a single one left; that belonging to the Prior of St. Gerold. And it was the same with the rest of the province; the reason being, of course, that the Arlberg railway had immensely reduced the price of wine from Lower Austria or South Tyrol, which used formerly to be imported by carrier, at great expense, over the Arlberg pass. Why cultivate bad wine, when you can buy a better quality for the same money?

The tunnel might have done something, he agreed, and so might the modern rise of industrialism hereabouts which tempted men from the fields into the factories; but the real reason was the change of climate. It had grown not colder, but damper. He was fond of wine; he had paid particular attention to this matter all his life; there could be no doubt about it. Feldkirch was a case in point. All its slopes were covered with vineyards not long ago; the Feldkirchers had grown so attached to their home product that they preferred it to anything from abroad. There was now not a vine left at Feldkirch. The grapes refused to ripen properly there, as they still did in more favored localities like Sulz-Röthis.[33]

---

[33] Since then, the same reason has been given me by two other natives, both of whom are in a position to know. I call it "interesting," because observations of a recent change of climate—and always in the direction of moisture—have been recorded in other parts of Europe. In the Shetland Islands, for instance, they will point out to you stretches of moor and heather once covered with grain which, owing to increased dampness, could no longer be got to mature. The same phenomenon has struck me also, but, on thinking it over, I attributed it to my own imagination; hot summers, I said to myself, and clear snowy winters, are far more likely to impress a child than rainy weather; hence we conclude rashly that in the days of our youth the climate was more continental. Yet how explain a state of affairs like this: vines were cultivated here by the Romans (even during the Stone Age, among the pile-dwellers on Lake Constance) and, assiduously, as early as the eleventh century; in 1615, again, there were no less than *one hundred vineyards at Bludesch alone.* The site of all of them is now nothing but grassy slopes. Can hay be more remunerative than wine? If not, there is perhaps something to be said for the change-of-climate theory. They

Thereafter we took the train to Bregenz. Hardly were we seated in our carriage before Mr. R. began:

"Now I want to know exactly what he said. Please repeat it."

"We were talking about the former production of wine in this province. He maintains that owing to recent climatic changes——"

"Not your old man! My old man."

Could anybody have remembered that rigmarole? I had to invent another one, at the end of which he said:

"So that was it? How sad, and how suggestive. The ravings of a mind diseased. Poor man! I must have that all down, word for word, in my diary...."

Despite Adelaide Procter's sprightly verses and its own illustrious ancestry, Bregenz remains a repulsive little town on the shore of its dead lake; and associated in my mind with infantile earaches and spankings. I went there not for fun, but for a set purpose; firstly, to consult the Curator of the new Museum, who was described as a prodigiously amiable person, as to what natural curiosities, if any, had lately been discovered in our upland regions, to re-inspect a picture, a sugary-watery Ganymede attributed to Angelika Kauffmann, left to this institution by my sister's will, a Roman votive stone found on my maternal grandfather's estate and other objects here deposited by members of my family, and to see whether his library contained any unknown works by old Theodor (or Thomas) Bruhin; secondly, to apply for the same object to that venerable convent-school of Mehrerau, where some homeward-bound Pope expired long ago and where, according to one of Bruhin's pamphlets, he was "Professor" and may well have left some documentary traces; thirdly, to visit the "Archiv" which contains a goodly collection of books, old and new, dealing with this province, and therefore, possibly, something of my father's, and also to refresh my memory in the matter of local dialects, place-names and so forth, and inspect early prints of places like

---

seem to have been gay people, by the way, in those bibulous days. Many are the complaints of illicit dancing and outrageous swearing, of "Versoffenheit und Tabakfressen"—drunkenness and tobacco-chewing.

Jagdberg, Blumenegg and Jordan-schloss; lastly, to present myself at the offices of the Alpine Club in order to go through the files of their "Mitteilungen" and make a list of my father's contributions to that journal, and see whether it contains some "Nachruf" of him, some obituary notice, as is likely enough, seeing that so tragic an accident to a conspicuous member can hardly have been left unrecorded.

A reasonable program.

I did none of these things; no, not one. Zeal for such scholarly investigations seems to be abating; or can it have been the weather? It happened to be cloudless. Much pleasanter, bathing in the lake and climbing up, towards evening, to admire the view from St. Gebhard's chapel.

We managed to go, none the less, to the Protestant cemetery which lies on the site of the *thermae* of old Brigantium, and examined the graves of no less than ten deceased relatives. Here lies, among the rest, that maternal grandfather who was responsible for the spankings aforesaid. His tombstone recounts his glories, and I do not believe in all of them; he doubtless had the memorial engraved half a century before his death, in order that posterity should make no mistake as to his merits while alive. This old feudal monster never did a stroke of work in his endless life. He was a braggart of the first water, with gray mustache that looked freshly waxed and curled—quite *à la* Münchhausen—at whatever hour of the day you might meet him; he radiated good health, and seemed everlastingly to have stepped that very moment out of a hot bath and the hands of a conscientious valet; he had a pink baby-complexion, and the candid eyes of the born liar. He spanked me as often as I came here in childhood, even as he had spanked his only son who died in youth—perhaps from the effects of it. Only once did I score off him during this earlier period. It was his unvarying habit to begin breakfast—a huge cup of a certain kind of chocolate, specially imported from Paris, for himself; tea or coffee for all the rest, and be damned to them—with a boiled egg. One morning of All Fool's Day I slipped down just before the others, devoured his egg, and turned the hollow shell upside down in its cup. On taking his seat, he had his customary whack at the seemingly sound egg: empty! He glowered round the table at a cluster of trembling daughters. At last he caught my eye and grunted:

"H'm. First of April, I presume. H'm. Not bad for a kid. H'm. Let me advise you to try that on somebody else, next year. H'm."

Even in later times, he continued to annoy me furiously by calling me a beetle-collector. This is how he talked:

"At seventeen, my lad, I was already commanding a fortress in Hungary. And here you are, catching cockroaches. Then we went to Greece with King Otho and ah! the lovely years we had there; the best of all my life! I was the first person to make excavations on the Acropolis of Athens, if you happen to have heard of such a place. Just make a note of that, young fellow. Meanwhile, here you are, hunting bugs and pinning labels to them. Afterwards—yes, Windsor! When I was aide-de-camp to your Prince Consort, he confessed that he could never have handled Victoria the way he did, unless I had told him (lowering his voice) some of my own experiences with capricious females of that class. *And here you are——*"

A fragment of the Greek yarn was true. He was there for long under Otho, roving about with his soldiers, and that forlorn and devastated country, as it then was, made an indelible impression on him. Not Odysseus himself could have been more homesick for Greece than he was. He spoke of it in tones of wistful yearning, as of a lost Paradise—the identical tones that I have since discovered, to my surprise, in the writings of a French contemporary, Edgar Quinet.[34] Never was he so

---

[34] I have just gone through Quinet's pages again. They are a thing apart, in French travel-literature. Here is no affectation, no mockery, no rhetoric, no complaints about this or that, no advice to the Greeks as to how they should govern themselves; nothing but the impressions of a blithe and sympathetic traveler. So he wanders through this country which then possessed "not a single two-wheeled carriage" nor domestic beasts of any kind; he gives us poignant sketches of its utter desolation—the fire-blackened villages and their few, half-starved inhabitants, the putrefying corpses, skeletons by the wayside, leagues of burnt forest and olive-groves; together with a few brighter descriptions of life in Arcadia, of those delightful Albanian children, and of chance meetings with the great Kolokotroni and others. What strikes me as distinctively non-French in Quinet is his whole-hearted love of nature, and a certain organic nobility of outlook. One would gladly quote from those stimulating reflections on the art of ancient

attractive, during these final years of his life, as when he sat all alone at the piano in the twilight hour before the lamps were brought in, crooning the tender Greek folk-songs of his youth to a soft, self-invented accompaniment. At such moments, he was transported; he had entered into a fairyland of which he alone possessed the key. You might have taken him for an angel. Indeed, his voice was the best part of him at all times. Even when he ramped and raved, it never lost its exquisite sweetness of timbre; his very curses sounded like a ripple of celestial laughter. He also painted sunny landscapes in oil, and composed an amusing valse or two. Such things went well with his exterior childlike equipment. Primeval ferocity was lurking underneath.

True to his freebooter instincts, he had perched himself here, at Bregenz, on a height where he could not be overlooked by any one and whence he obtained an unimpeded view of half the province and lake. The place boasted of a "flag-tower" from which five countries were visible (Austria, Bavaria, Wurtemberg, Baden and Switzerland), and he contrived, somehow or other, to give a mediæval smack of discord and rapine to its inner regions. Here were bleak stone passages, cold as an ice-cellar in winter, and hung with matchlocks and lances; gloomy Gothic wardrobes filling up their ends. The habitable part was full of spoils plundered, without a doubt, from the rich burghers down below; a haphazard collection of Persian carpets, harmoniums, lacquer tables, Tiepolo portraits,

---

Greece, but as I am on the subject of homesickness, I will merely transcribe what he says of Sparta (then a mere hovel) which has the true nostalgic ring. "Je laisse à d'autres à expliquer comment une ville qui ne vous est rien, bien moins, quelques tertres de cailloux que vous ne reverrez jamais, peuvent vous manquer plus que votre terre natale." Quinet, it will be seen, wrote as citizen of the world, not of France; and that is why his book is a thing apart. It ends with a touching farewell to the whole country. "Ni demain, ni après, ne verrai-je plus mes hôtes de Dhervény ou de Mistra, ni les forêts brulées, ni les os sur la grève, ni tout ce que les hommes peuvent souffrir pour une pensée, sans cesser de la mettre à haut prix ..."
There once passed through my hands a copy of these travels marginally annotated by some Greek reader in faded, yellow ink. One of his observations ran to this effect: "Ce livre est tout ce qu'il doit être, admirable de description et de vérité. Moi, Grec, je puis témoigner que ce livre est plein de vérités et de charmes."

glittering chandeliers, marbles: it all wore an authentic air of loot. Somber paneling, relieved by armorial designs, covered the walls and ceilings and made the rooms uncommonly dusky.

And here he sat for years and years, terrorizing his family, all females, into fits. People used to wonder how he managed to look so absurdly young at eighty. His secret was simplicity itself: Live well, and hand over everything in the way of worry to your women. He never spoke to servants at all; the harim were entrusted with that dirty work, and woe betide them if anything went wrong with the dinner! No one was surprised when his five daughters got engaged as fast as ever they could and fled the premises, regardless of whom they were marrying. He ruled his wife and sister-in-law, dear old ladies, like a slave-driver. One or the other was always hard at work manufacturing Latakia cigarettes for the rosy brigand, who lived on their money for seventy years and called them names to the hour of his death, although they were children of the premier baron of Scotland. A certain daughter had the imprudence, one day, to admire a graceful birch-tree that she could see from her bedroom. Next morning, as usual, she looked out of the window; the birch was gone. It had been felled overnight. That was his system. Dominate your women, or they will dominate you. Put the fear of God into them—no matter how. In his own family, he declared, wives were not allowed to sit down in the presence of their husbands, unless they had first obtained permission. It may be true. I fancy one of his ancestors was the cosmopolitan ruffian who wrote those memoirs; a kind of fifth-rate Casanova. There he remained, anyhow, like an old cock on his dunghill, crowing and gobbling; vicious and vigorous past his ninetieth year. And the strange thing is that I am considered to have inherited a great deal of his peculiar charm. It was my mother who told me this; she was his eldest daughter and knew both of us fairly well.

It is time, now, to confess that not all the prints and archives and natural history collections in the world would have brought me—or ought to bring any one else—to Bregenz, did the place not offer another and a greater attraction. I am alluding to the local *Blaufelchen* whose English name at this moment escapes me: a kind of fish. They are called, in Latin, *Coregonus Wartmanni*, which has a harsh flavor. Let nobody, however, be scared by a mere name, inasmuch as things are apt to taste different from what they sound. Oriental poets, for example, have sung with such a depth of feeling about pomegranates that one almost believes they can be eaten, whereas *Coregoni Wartmanni*, I admit, convey a suggestion of something unpalatable. Try them none the less, and leave Hafiz to crack his teeth over the pomegranates.

These fish occur in some Scotch lakes and are considered so great a delicacy that Mary Queen of Scots has been credited with their introduction. But I knew one cantankerous countryman of mine (an angler, and *Coregonus* will not rise to the fly) who declared that they were "not to be compared to trout"—which means nothing whatever, seeing that comparison is not well possible between things so dissimilar; you might as well say that Sir Joshua Reynolds is not to be compared to a Bechstein Grand; and that, in fact, they were "hardly worth eating"—which has the merit, at least, of being a straightforward expression of opinion. Now it stands to reason that a good many things are hardly worth eating, until you know how to cook them. The average English hare is hardly worth eating; the way that quadruped is "dressed" (hyperbola!) in England is an insult to the hare's memory and to the human stomach. As to these *Blaufelchen*—whoever does not approve of them at the Hotel Weisses Kreuz in Bregenz must be hard to please.[35] Let him try, as a last resort, those at the Hotel Hecht in Constance; if still dissatisfied, he should return without delay to his lukewarm whitebait fried in mutton-grease.

But, first of all, a word for your guidance. Make love neither to the waitress nor the chamber-maid nor the she-cook. Make love to the manager. Lure him into some corner, and unbosom yourself freely. Whisper in his ear that you are an Ainu by birth; that while out there, at Yezo, you accidentally met a countryman of his (mentioning name and general appearance) who spoke in such glowing terms of the Bodensee *Blaufelchen* that you were unable to sleep either by

---

[35] Avoid the lake salmon.

day or night until, traveling via the trans-Siberian railway, you should be able to taste them for yourself under his hospitable roof. Then see whether you get what is "hardly worth eating." I blush to record that we had a veritable surfeit of *Blaufelchen*. I devoured two at a sitting, and the waitress informed me that she had never seen a tourist—even a German—perform a similar feat; nor should I, indeed, have been successful, had I not kept saying to myself all the time: "When shall I be at Bregenz again? Possibly never!" Mr. R. declared himself satisfied with one; and small wonder. It was a leviathan....

A timely warning, apropos of surfeits. On arrival at our village, we found the family in a state of distress. One of their two cows (the rest are on the alp) had died that afternoon; died of over-eating. She, the proprietress, had told him, the proprietor, to beware how he left the beast to itself; he, the proprietor, swore he had known that particular cow from the day of its birth, and that it was far more sensible than the rest of its kind. Left to itself, therefore, the cow had "exploded."

I am so little of a cattle-fancier that this was news to me; troubling news. I had always regarded the cow as an exemplar of all that is sane and moderate. Far from it. Give them a chance, especially after the hay-diet of winter, and they eat till they burst. They graze, and graze, and graze; at last, stuffed to the brim, they stand there motionless, wondering what is wrong inside, while a pained and puzzled look—infallible symptom, this—creeps into their eyes. Now is your chance, your last chance, of saving their life. If you happen to have an iron chain in your pocket, thrust it into the beast's mouth to provoke a flow of saliva or something else which relieves the oppression; if you have no chain look in that other pocket, where you may find a Gargantuan clyster to be applied to its further extremity; failing that, whip out your butcher's knife and give the patient a well-directed stab in the stomach—a kind of Cæsarian section; the gas escapes, the cow survives. Else, after standing like a pathetic statue for a few moments, it falls heavily earthwards and "explodes inside"—a cow! Thank God we belong to another species, else how would it have fared at the Weisses Kreuz? A gentle cow! The episode has shattered one of my dearest illusions.

This, then, must be the explanation of a strange sight which has attracted me from time immemorial. Often, in pouring rain, you may see a cow at pasture and its owner standing dismally near at hand, soaked to the skin. Why, I used to wonder—why not let the beast graze by itself and go home and get a *Schnapps* and a change of clothes? Now I know. The peasant cannot move from the spot. He dare not leave the cow alone. He must stay there and keep his eye fixed on hers, lest that symptom should appear.

OLD ANNA

STOOD awhile yesterday beside a block of gneiss which projects upon the right-hand side of the Tiefis path, some two hundred yards above the petrifying stream, at the foot of a young oak. It has been broken long ago, and is shaped like a very low and narrow bench. How one changes—how one looks at things with other eyes! Is it possible that this stone used to be my *Ultima Thule* in days of infancy; this, or the walnut tree a little higher up, whose stump remains to this day, and from under whose branches you had a broad view over the valley? The upward path was shadier than now, and here, sure enough, I played through the morning hours, while the old Anna extracted out of her pocket that invariable *Frühschoppen* (she, being Tyrolese, called it "merenda")—some salted bread and a quarter of red wine. Sometimes the same pocket produced also a chocolate for me; in fact, she had a trick of conjuring chocolate out of the most improbable places. On one occasion she actually shook a piece down from a tree; a miracle....

Later on, the Gleziska became our favorite haunt. This is a flat green meadow to the east of the village where stood, at that time, a glorious barn containing an ante-chamber and two separate compartments full of delicious hay to swim about in; it has now been replaced by an anæmic structure of the new type. The first walk I ever took, all by myself, was from the village church to the Gleziska; that was a proud day. Soon, when my sister had learnt to toddle, the old thing took us further afield; once as far as the church of St. Martin at Ludesch (built about 1430; some of its rare Gothic furniture is in the Bregenz Museum), where we two discovered, in a crypt, an immense accumulation of human skulls; we dragged four or five into the daylight, and had a game of skittles with them.

I still own a photograph of the old Anna. She is not old in the least; about forty, I should say. There she sits at a table, half-profile, her left arm supporting the head; she does not smile, but looks rather vacuously into the world, as such photographs are apt to do. A pleasant, refined face; I can read nothing else out of it. There is a suggestion of silk about the clothing, and a black ribbon hangs down from the back of her hair. Such was the *Alte Anna* who, being a child of nature herself, was the ideal nurse.

Her only drawback was that she had too great a fondness for ghastly wolf-stories of the Little Red Riding Hood type. She possessed an endless store of such tales current, no doubt, in the Tyrol of earlier days. I wish I could still remember them, for they would now interest me as showing how strongly the popular imagination must have been impressed with this scourge, at which we can at last afford to laugh. In those days they frightened me to death; they haunted my dreams.

Old Anna faded out of sight, and there came a shadowy interregnum of German governesses, of whom I can recall nothing save that a certain Fräulein Schubert got the sack because she had a flirtation (this was doubtless a euphemism) with some young man in the factory offices. It struck me as unfair that you should be sent away just because you happen to like your friend.

Herr Som followed. He was master of the boys' school at Bludesch (there was no school-house in our village at that time); a Swiss, I fancy, and a well-groomed, gentlemanly fellow who often lunched at our house. To his establishment I was now sent every morning—rather a long tramp for a child, across all those fields, especially through the fresh-fallen snow of winter. The school-house still exists; it is a conspicuous three-storied building that overtops all the others in this hither side of Bludesch; a house of noble lineage which has recently been made to look quite new and respectable; it was built in the seventeenth century by the family of Von der Halden zu Haldenegg, who were *Landvogts* of Blumenegg.[36] The place was therefore not a school-house at all; only two rooms had been set apart by the village elders where boys sat at desks under Herr Som's supervision writing in endless lines "Schwimmmmen, Schwimmmen" (it was spelt with four, or at least three, m's in those days). Som must have been pleased with my progress, for I still possess a unique document—a school report with the mark "very good" in reading, writing and

---

[36] They are buried at Bludesch—the last one in 1669—in that crypt below the church which bears the awesome superscription: *Fui non sum. Estis non critis.* They also built what is now the Krone inn at that village, one of whose ceilings has taken refuge in the Bregenz Museum, and whose present proprietor was a schoolfellow of mine at Som's.

arithmetic; so pleased that, on marrying soon afterwards, he gave my exotic name to his eldest son, the first and last time such an honor has been conferred on me. "Schwimmmmen" is all that sticks in my mind of Bludesch school; that, and the view up the smiling valley from the window of the water-closet (another euphemism). It was then and there borne in upon me how needful to such apartments is a spacious prospect upon which the eye can dwell with pleasure. To this attraction I should be inclined to add, now, a choice little library and, for those of musical tastes, a pianola.

Misguided Scotch relatives, in those days, used to send magnificent dolls to my sister by post. Little they knew what they were doing: little they knew! A parcel arrived, and somebody would say to her:

"Well, I declare. This looks uncommonly like another doll. *Another* doll! You are a lucky child, and no mistake."

My sister pretended to shriek delightedly:

"Oh, let me unpack it, all alone, upstairs," and snatched away the parcel and ran. I followed. A glance, a single masonic glance, had been exchanged between us. It sufficed. I knew the part I was called upon to play.

Upstairs, in some unused room, we locked the door upon our labors. The plaything was unpacked in dead silence; a ceremonial had begun. When the last silk-paper wrapping had been removed, my sister took the splendid golden-haired creature into her arms and, with many false hugs and kisses, bore it swiftly towards the garden. I followed. Not a word was spoken. We were high priests, engaged upon some terrible but necessary ordinance. At the foot of a certain old tree in a certain shrubbery—always the same—she paused, and muttered certain mysterious words into the victim's ear. Then she handed it solemnly to me. I took the thing by the legs, swung it through the air once or twice, and shattered its head to fragments against the trunk. After that, we tore it limb from limb amid a shower of sawdust and stamped on the remains. Forthwith the spell was released, the sacrifice at an end; and we screamed with hysterical joy.

A few days later, somebody might enquire of the child:

"Now where is that lovely doll you got from dear Cousin Annie?"

She would reply, mournfully:

"In bed. Poor little Esmeralda has a tummy-ache this morning."

This, too, was part of the rite. The words were always the same.

Never a doll escaped assassination, and nobody, I believe, found out what happened to them. My sister hated dolls with a vindictive, unreasoning hatred. And I, of course, was only too pleased to smash anything I was bidden to smash; and still am.

Dear Cousin Annie—this one happened to be no relation at all—turned up in this country at odd intervals, as did the rest of those stark grand-aunts and female cousins, to our infinite annoyance. There were scores of them, and all of a kind; musty and sententious to the last degree. The present generation has no idea, not the faintest idea, of what a grand-aunt used to look like in those days. Dear Cousin Annie was a gaunt, tottering, gray-haired anatomy, who reeked of Macassar oil, and wore massive jet beads round her neck and a tremulous drop of rose-water at the end of her nose—just the kind of person whom a little boy would love to kiss.

"What is my name, dear?" she asked, over and over again, with a sickly smile.

You were expected to answer:

"Dear—Cousin—Annie."

It was no use whatever saying, "Don't know." We tried it often, but the question was only repeated with greater persistence, and a sicklier smile than ever.

Her husband had been a physician and was even more aged than she; he exhaled an air of unbelievable eld. It occurred to me, years afterwards, that there was something pre-Victorian and Waterlooish about those white whiskers. He drank sherry-wine, and dishes of tea. Nevertheless, one could have learnt much from him had one been a little older, for he was a character, an original. Later on, in Edinburgh, I got to know him well; he was then ninety-two, and no longer communicative. An antiquarian of the old school, he had filled his head with queer knowledge upon every subject, and his house with queer objects of every kind. Judging by his pamphlets and letters to newspapers, he seems to have taken, and rightly taken, all learning to his province. I still possess a few of these things;

who can tell how many he produced altogether? "Protestantism in Austria" begins thus: "I am desirous of calling the attention of your readers to this subject, which is not generally understood in Britain." It was written here, as well as a rather incoherent "Notice of a flood at Frastanz in the autumn of 1846."[37] He gave me another paper written by his own father, who was Fellow of the Royal College of Surgeons and died in 1818: "Mistresses and Servants." How good it reads!

B. My dear Mrs. A., I am glad to see you. All well at home, I hope?

A. All well. Mr. A. is going about in his usual way, and the children are in good health.

B. When things are so, a wife and mother may truly say: "He gives all things richly to enjoy."

So far *all well*; but Mrs. A. promptly embarks upon her pet subject of "plaguy servants." Mrs. B., after an argument of sixteen pages, recommends her to read a certain verse in St. Paul's Epistle to the Ephesians.

Here is a short paper of his own on "Saints" ("When I was student at the University of Edinburgh, we young fellows were displeased by our professor, a worthy old man, constantly speaking to us of *Baron* Haller"), and a strange composition touching the "Life of a domestic cat". ("I kept a record of her kittenings. They were twenty-five in number, comprising seventy-eight individuals.") The old fellow also burst into poetry once or twice and perpetrated, among other things, some flattering lines on our family of Tilquhillie entitled "Feugh and Dee," lines which nothing but ingrained modesty now prevents me from reprinting, seeing that this family, though venerable enough—the oldest in the county, they tell me—was never yet, to my knowledge, hymned in verse, but has contrived to live on, from age to age, sufficiently inconspicuous; inconspicuous, and all of us rather cracked into the bargain. See, for a recent example, Dean Ramsay's "Reminiscences."

Thereafter came an epoch when those in authority seem to

---

[37] Frastanz is famous for its beer and for its battle, on Saturday, 20 April, 1499, between the Swiss and the Imperial troops, which seems to have been the bloodiest ever fought in this province. There is a pretty legend connected with it (*see* Vonbun's "Sagen Vorarlbergs," Innsbruck, 1858).

have reached a sensible conclusion, to wit, that English children should not only speak English, but also learn to read and write it. A governess was required. In due course of time she arrived; and her name was Miss Prime. We straightway called her Miss Prim, or "the Prim"; it suited her admirably. Her hair was parted down the middle; indeed, she was prim all over, but her pedagogic system proved a failure. Miss Prim must have had an indifferent time of it here, so far as the children were concerned. Her disciplinary measures never obtained the desired effect. When my sister was told to stand on a bench for some misdemeanor, she made such contortions at me that it was impossible for lessons to proceed; she was next put into a corner facing the wall, where the contortions continued more violently than ever, only this time with the back part of her body; at last she was locked up all by herself in a distant room, whence there presently issued such a din of crashing furniture that the people downstairs rushed up, asking whether the end of the world had come. In this particular room stood an enormous double bed; it inspired her with a brilliant method of eluding punishment for good and all.

"Crawl under here," she suggested, "whenever the Prim want us *for anything* (euphemism). She can never pull us out."

She couldn't. Under that bed we remained for hours, contentedly munching cakes and crunching sweets which had been stuffed into the mattress to meet contingencies such as these, until the Prim implored us, almost on her knees, to come out again. At other times, before or after "lessons," we indulged in prolonged and uproarious fights between ourselves. "It will end in a howl," my mother was wont to remark on such occasions.

Nobody need tell me what we required: a thorough good spanking. Who was going to administer it? Had my father not died when I was five, he would doubtless have attended to the matter. He could hurt confoundedly, he could. I have bright memories of one of his spankings when, after performing a war-dance on some bed of newly planted portulacas, I found myself suddenly seized by the scruff of the neck and carried at arm's length rabbit-fashion, dangling and kicking in air, into a conservatory. *En route*, I had barely time to shout to the old Anna "Wait till I'm spanked!"—we were going for a walk—

before I got it hotter, far hotter, than usual. That is the way to spank children. Never do it unless you are really angry yourself. Otherwise they will regard you as a cold-blooded torturer.

As to the Prim—I should like to have seen her tackling either of us two seriously. Even my sister, tiny as she was, would have throttled her to death, and then dropped her out of the window. She was regarded as a poor joke, and that is why her teaching hardly met with the success it deserved, and why I was therefore soon to be sent to an English private school, loathsomest of institutions, and thence to other schools, and yet other schools—there to be crammed for such a length of time with such a superfluity of useless learning, and by such a variety of unwholesome-looking gentlemen of different ages and nationalities, that I am only now, at the end of all these years, beginning to shake off the bad effects and discover my true self again. That fetish of education!

Meanwhile Miss Prim, during one of her holiday visits to England, had succeeded in getting engaged. She imparted the happy news to our family, with becoming shyness, a few hours after her return; she wondered whether her fiancé might ever come out here, and proceed with his courtship on foreign soil, for a week or so? Why, of course he could; let him come when he pleased, and stay as long as ever he liked! In due course of time he arrived; and his name was Mr. Clutterbuck. Clutterbuck. Clutterbuck. The name alone sent us into fits; we thought it an incomparably funny one, as indeed it is. Mr. Clutterbuck, himself, was a droll and pertinacious individual. He used to sit, rod in hand, trying to catch trout in the reservoirs. Everybody told him he would never get a nibble there—the fish were far too well-fed; why not try a fly on the Tabalada stream, at the bottom of the valley near Gais, the fishing of which also belonged to us?

No. Mr. Clutterbuck preferred the reservoirs. He would sit on that stone margin morning and afternoon, while the Prim hovered lovingly in his neighborhood. There I see him sitting to this day.

The only way to get these pampered beasts out of the

reservoir is by the prosaic method of draining off the water. Then you have them! Now just remove your trousers and wade into the mud, if you do not mind looking like a fool, and pull them out with your hands, which is far more exciting sport than you might imagine. Only then is it possible to realize how slippery and muscular a trout can be when taken, not off a hook after an hour's playing, but fresh from its element. We used to do this periodically in later years, and some of the fish were of respectable size. The largest I remember catching weighed a fraction over four kilograms and was seventy-six centimeters in length. He kicked like an electric dynamo.

We happened to be going that afternoon to a friend in Bregenz and decided to make him a present of this trout, particularly as he had a far-famed Viennese *chef* who claimed to be able to make a succulent ragout out of the Devil himself. As there was no time for a special box to be built, we requisitioned the newly made coffin of a child that had died overnight but was happily not yet bestowed therein; our monster was packed inside, comfortably wrapped up in green nettles. The baby could wait; the trout was in a hurry....

SCHLINS

THERE is a sense of sudden departure in the air.

We shall know the worst, to-morrow, or next day....

Lasko's well has not moved from its old place. It lies about a hundred yards west of the "Château aux fenêtres." The wooden trough into which the water trickles—one of its many successors—looks the same as ever; I am glad it has not yet been converted into a basin of cement, like those in the village below.

The transformation of wood into cement is proceeding relentlessly all over the country; to my infinite disgust. Those numerous wooden watertroughs for the use of householders and their cattle, which used to be quite a feature of the streets, are now all being manufactured out of this damnably durable material; there is a cement-factory near our station, and I wish somebody would drop a bomb on it. Cement has invaded domestic architecture, as was inevitable. Inevitable things are not always pleasant, and not always pretty. It is hard to imagine anything more infamous, on a small scale, than the prison-like gray garden walls which have replaced those delightful wooden palings through whose meshes a riot of flowers would come tumbling out upon the road; the spacious wooden houses, so full of charm and individuality, so redolent of patriarchal well-being, with their shingles and gables burnt to a glowing umber-brown by years and years of sunshine, are being discarded in favor of weedy little cement abominations that make one sorry for people who have to live in them. They look cheap; they are cheap. I wish they were dear, for cheap things are seldom attractive, and life in cheap and ugly homes cannot fail to give their inmates a corresponding bent of mind.

Not a single wooden bridge is left over Lutz or Ill. They were swept away, every one of them, in the floods of 1910 and 1911 and now, for the first time, their place is taken by solid but hideous structures of cement. One is sorry to let the old ones go; one calls to mind the bridge at Ludesch built as long ago as 1498 and ever since then kept in repair, with its sloping wooden roof, its sudden twilight within and odor of hot fir-wood, as of a scented tunnel; one remembers the soft tread of the horses' feet on the powdery beams and the sound of creaking timbers underfoot. They are eyesores, these new things; they will remain eyesores.

Now a new road is an eyesore too, ruthlessly hacked, as it is, through the landscape; and nearly every road hereabouts, great or small, has been cut afresh within the last generation. No great harm in this, however, since roads have a knack of growing old again; you need only wait; lichens and grass and brushwood will presently creep up to hide the scars. There is nothing to be done with palings and bridges and troughs and houses of cement; nothing, save to stand aside and curse them. For the æsthetic drawback of cement, that godsend to lazy builders, lies in its agelessness and lack of character; if it grows old at all, it grows even more horrible than in youth. But men are becoming blind to these and other uglifications—the word is not quite ugly enough for the thing—of the scenery and of their houses. For instance: forty-one unseemly electric wires converge at the post-office of our small village; there they are, so repulsive that you cannot but look at them; the women of the place, instead of feeding chickens or mending the children's clothes, spend their lives in gossiping with each other at long distances, and God alone knows the nonsense they find to chatter about. Go where you please, in fact, and you cannot fail to perceive half a dozen decorative telegraph poles staring you in the face. Now why do people want all this ridiculous electricity rushing up and down the country? Solidarity. Brotherhood of men....

Lasko's well——

No; it has not moved from its old place. But we looked in vain for those "Wasserkälber" which were always to be found lying at its bottom in olden days. Indeed, I have not seen a single "Wasserkälb" since my arrival here. Are they extinct?[38]

We called him Lasko; but it was not till many years afterwards, at an English public school, that I learnt that Lasko really meant anything. And we called it Lasko's well, because it was here that Lasko, our black retriever, lapped up some water

---

[38] These "water-calves" are thin, wire-like worms of the family of the Gordiidae; they pass through singular stages of development. We used to be told blood-curdling tales of their effects on the human stomach if accidentally swallowed with the water.

on his last walk, the day before his death. After that, we made it a rule that every one of our dogs, as often as we passed this place, should drink at the trough in memory of dear old Lasko, whether he happened to be thirsty or not; if he refused, his head was held under the water till he had imbibed, willy-nilly, something like the requisite amount of liquid. To this treatment were submitted:

(1) Lasko the Second, a worthless yellow brute who, having been altered in youth, was of so timorous a disposition that it became our greatest delight to get somebody to fire off a gun in his immediate neighborhood, and watch him flee for his life.

(2) Sippins, who belonged to my sister and to the "Affenpincher" breed—that is, to so small and strange-looking a canine variety that the boys were wont to call him a Chinese rat; all of which did not prevent him from having fleas. One wonders whether those enthusiasts, who declare that dogs have no fleas, are in earnest. Have they ever looked for them? Sippins was flea'd, during the summer, twice a day by a maid who deposited the insects in a saucer containing alcohol, and in my boyish journal I record "136 fleas caught from Sippins at a single time"—Sippins himself, as aforesaid, being about the size of a full-grown rat. Now Sippins objected strongly to this water-cure at Lasko's well. He had been born and educated at Munich; he only touched water when no beer was procurable; he could drink like a lord, like a fish; but only beer. It was not long, therefore, before it became one of our principal pastimes to "make Sippins drunk." He seldom knew when to stop.

(3) MacDougall, a Skye-terrier belonging to me, of so pure a breed that you never knew whether he was walking forwards or backwards. He was an anomaly among quadrupeds; nothing approaching his style had been seen in this country before. His talent consisted in enticing cats down from walls and trees and other inaccessible situations by his mere appearance; the cats, seemingly, being unable to resist the temptation of inspecting at close quarters this freak of nature, this animated hearth-rug. Once on the ground, they were doomed to a violent death, for they never dreamt it was a dog. Need I say what our chief diversion with MacDougall used to be? One of his most brilliant exploits took place in Bludesch at our tailor's—who was also

our haircutter; whence, for many years, I found it difficult to realize that tailoring and haircutting were separate professions—where dwelt a family of cats, a mother and half a dozen kittens. The operation took less than a minute to perform, while we looked on amazed and, ten to one, amused; two shakes for the mother, half a shake each for the kittens; the entire family laid out flat on the grass, dead as doornails, side by side; whereupon he trotted up to us, right end forward, saying plainly: "*How's that?*" And we doubtless replied: "Oh, MacDougall! Do it again." Very cruel children, we were....

Straight up, from Lasko's well, and once more to that inspiring portal of green, where the path to Tiefis enters the cavern-like forest. To-day those curtain-fringes of the dark firs are waving softly to and fro, stirred by a tepid Fön wind. Now down again, past sundry erratic blocks and through the newly planted tract to the "nymphe pudique"—the source of the crayfish stream, which we intend to pursue all the way to Schlins. A good deal of that fair swamp growth has been cut since our last visit; enough remains to please the eye. The vale grows wider after the Tiefis-Bludesch road has been crossed, and the rushes denser; one realizes why the peasants have called this rivulet "Ried-bach." It meanders in desultory fashion about this upper marshy level; then plunges, all of a sudden, into the wood, and puts on a new character. A downhill career begins in earnest. Rapids are formed, and islets; all in the deep shade of those trees through which it glimmers obscurely along. A kingfisher haunts these dusky reaches (there is another on the upper Montiola brook); scenery such as this must have been in Poe's mind when he wrote "The Island of the Fay." Soon we pass a small abandoned reservoir; it is the second spot in the district where bulrushes can be found—the third is near Bludenz; after that comes a stretch of country difficult to follow, steep and irregular, a stretch of tortuous windings and cascades, till the lower level of Schlins is reached, where the brook enters upon its final phase, gliding demurely, like our own Feldbächle, through cultivated meadows at the foot of Jagdberg.

It stands to reason that we straightway found ourselves sitting at the Krone inn, wistful at the thought that this might be our last visit here. The proprietress is a sweet-natured woman and a stimulating conversationalist; we talked and talked, while

Mr. R. partook of his traditional two eggs and insisted moreover in drinking "Suser," freshly made cider, in spite of my warning about the probable consequences of such rash behavior, namely, an attack of the "Holde Katarina," the "Fair Katherine," which signifies a loosening of the bowels. The expression is remarkable as showing the prudishness of these folk in regard to bodily matters of every kind; alter a letter in that name, and you may divine its origin. All such things are slurred over, even by grown-up people. So female dogs are always known as "he"; incredible to relate, our much-married dachshund-lady is "he." How different from Mediterranean countries where sexuality and every other physiological fact is taken for granted by the smallest children, and emphasized as such; where even inanimate objects are apt to be invested with the attributes of sex! Here we stand before a racial divergence of outlook; a gulf.

The cider-harvest promises well. But I have long ago given up pretending to enjoy this drink, and find it hard to believe that the first time I ever got tipsy was on such mawkish stuff. Yet so it was. Needless to say, it was not my own fault; other people were mixed up in the affair; Jakob, and my sister. Jakob was a smiling, sunburnt villager who looked after our cows and pigs and also helped at the hay-making; the accident, therefore, must have occurred at the present season of the year. Now whatever Jakob did, he did with such peculiar zest that it was a liberal education to watch him. Nobody could *dengel* quite like he could (to *dengel* is to beat out the blade of a scythe); he threw his heart and soul into the performance. And nobody could quaff cider with such infinite gusto; it made you thirsty to look at him. Wherever he happened to be mowing among the fields, there, close at hand, in the shade of some tree, stood his jug of blue stoneware out of which he refreshed himself gloriously, in god-like fashion, from time to time. When it was empty, he was wont to disappear down the stairs of the laundry into certain mysterious regions underneath our house and come back with the jug refilled; and this is where my sister's rôle begins. She was three years old at the time; the suggestion, therefore, can only have come from her; the suggestion, I mean, that we should watch where Jakob went and then get some cider for ourselves. It was another world down there, a cool twilight passage running the whole length of the house, with vaulted chambers on both sides that were lighted by windows ever so high up. One of them was full of barrels side by side, and one of those barrels was still dripping. Aha! So that was where Jakob filled his jug. Now just the least little turn of the tap, and the liquid began to trickle deliciously down our throats, while we egged each other on to drink more and more. I have no idea how long we stayed down there. The countryside was scoured in vain; all traces of the children had disappeared, and had it not been for Jakob providentially descending to fetch himself yet another jugful, we might have remained undiscovered till next morning. As it was, we were picked up senseless and put to bed.

Seven o'clock—how long one has lingered in this pleasant tavern! Now we leave, after many farewellings, and wander homewards due east, not passing the church at all; we cross the streamlet which has accompanied us hither and immediately enter that wood, familiar by this time, the once awe-inspiring forest of the——. It is already dark here, under the firs, but the rich, resinous perfumes of daylight are still hanging in the air; no dew has fallen to quench them. So we move along the dim path in silence; we have talked ourselves out, at Schlins.

All those squirrels—what has become of them? In olden days you could seldom traverse any wood hereabouts without encountering one or more. Now, during the whole of our stay here, we have seen but two; one black, one red. Where are they gone? I enquired, and learnt that they had not been persecuted during the war, as were the moles. To be sure, certain persons eat squirrels and declare them to be excellent; they did this already in the days when these animals were numerous. In England, also, the race seems to be dying out. Has there been some epidemic, or is the whole squirrel-tribe growing weary of life and contemptuous of the joys of propagation? Quite lonesome these forests are, without their squirrels. As to the crested tits—they seem to have vanished altogether; in fact, the entire titmouse tribe is far less common than it used to be. Have their nesting-places grown rarer or are they, too, becoming ascetic? We have wandered leagues and leagues about these woodlands, and not once have I heard that melodious trill; not once.

Out, into the odorous *pré des papillons*, into a fading, greenish-gray atmosphere, a kind of elf-land. All is moist here, and mysterious. An owl sallies forth on our left and circles twice directly overhead, so close that we can discern her eyes and beak. Then up through misty fields past a decrepit hay-hut, one of the survivors of the old school like that near the crayfish-stream, one of those whose planks are encrusted with sulphur-hued lichen. Now Mr. R. produces his talisman and plays as we walk in the gloaming; many new *morceaux* have been "found" since that day at Blumenegg. Our last concert, possibly! And just when I was beginning to appreciate, and even understand—which is far more difficult—this aboriginal music with its up-to-date names!

Marching along I review, in fancy, the many scenes which have lately flitted before our eyes, and one little memory creeps up among the throng; I think it will end in submerging them all. It was what we saw a few days ago during our latest stroll to the ruined Jagdberg. I make a point, namely, of losing myself on the way there (it is quite easy; you have only to bear a little to the north in the woods) because, in so doing, you never fail to see something, however insignificant, which you never saw before. So it fell out. We duly lost our way and, floundering down a thickly wooded incline, came to the margin of a small crescent-shaped bog, surrounded by old firs. It was as solitary a spot as you might wish to find; for all one knew, the foot of man had never trodden here. Now I have spoken of the many-tinted vegetation of these marshy tracts. This one, for reasons which a botanist may expound, was of another nature. It had been dedicated wholly to gentians.[39] They shot up from the wet moss—a blaze of the most perfect blue on earth. Theirs was not a steady light, but shimmering and playful, and of a luster so intense that no African sky, no sapphire, could have rivaled it. I plucked one of these portentous flowers. It measured nearly the

---

[39] *G. asclepiadea,* which the Germans briefly call "Schwalbenwurzblättriger Enzian." Old Conrad Gesner knew it as "poison-root," not because it was poisonous in itself, but because cattle were said to eat it in order to cure themselves of the stings of poisonous animals. He learnt this piece of lore, as well as the plant's popular name, from the botanist Aretius (Benedikt Marti), and therefore wished to call the flower "Aretia" in honor of him. Two hundred years later Haller, the great countryman of Aretius, did give the name Aretia to a certain genus of plants; and it was retained by Linné.

length of my walking-stick and was alive with color from end to end. Conceive a hundred thousand of them, all huddled together among those somber trees. We seemed to be looking down into a lake of blue fire.

Here, I think, is a memory to cherish; a vision to carry away into other lands.

Sunday, 3 September. Departure! We leave by the 1 a.m. train to-night.

And it would not be hard to guess where we went this afternoon, for a final stroll.

There, in the well-known room, was the "old one" as well as her husband, and the baby looking prettier than ever since her holiday at Thüringerberg; there also were some twenty other people, peasant-folk, chatting at tables, and smoking and drinking beer. Sunday! We had overlooked this fact. And there they would sit, till all hours of the night. "Not much chance of *embrassez-moi* in here," I thought, as I looked round. Mr. R. remained in the open doorway, and his disappointment took a tragic turn. He said bitterly:

"What are all our pleasant walks and talks worth now? Ah, I shall have nothing but unhappy memories of your country."

"That you shall not," I declared. "Nobody is to have unhappy memories of my country, if I can help it. Now this is a moment for heroic measures, and one little thing has just dawned upon me; what cannot be done inside a room, may be done outside. Let us sit down, while you order your eggs. I have it. I have it already. Those eggs.... How lucky you are fond of eggs. How lucky you have a friend who knows why eggs were created!"

We gave our orders.

"What on earth am I to do?" asked Mr. R.

"You will presently leave the room, without turning round to look at anybody. Go into the orchard at the back of the house, and wait there. When the baby arrives, I give you thirty seconds together. Employ them in a laughing and brotherly fashion, as I told you the other day. Then you, at least, will return straight here. Thirty seconds. If you mean to obey to the letter, swear it. Else no baby till the crack of doom. Now, swear."

Whereupon Mr. R. swore a great oath in the Mediterranean

manner, on the head, or the honor—on both, I fancy—of his own mother, to obey to the letter.

"Thirty seconds," I went on. "Imagine otherwise what might happen if the old one grew suspicious and went into the orchard! And she may well be suspicious, after those marconigrams of the other day. What would she think of us two conspirators? How about my reputation here, in the only country where, by good luck, I have not yet been found out; where my family name is a byword for all that is upright and honorable; where my father, my grandfather.... Just let me hear you swear again."

Whereupon he swore a second great oath, to the same effect as the first, on the souls of all his dead ancestors, male and female.

"Thirty seconds.... You can go now. And listen! Clasp her firmly if you get the chance, or you may bungle the whole affair, and these are the little accidents one never forgives oneself. After all, it would be a queer baby who objected to being embraced for thirty seconds by such an affectionate elder brother. Why should she?"

"I was going to do that anyhow."

He departed; and presently the fateful eggs arrived and remained on the table one minute, two minutes. I beckoned Dorothea to my side:

"Will you go and fetch my friend? His eggs are getting cold. You may find him in the orchard; he is fond of orchards. *Run!*" and I gave her a gentle push. Whether she perceived the strategy or not, she was off like an arrow.

What happened under those apple-trees I shall learn in due course of time, by the simple expedient of asking no questions. Up to this moment I only know that Mr. R. returned alone, and sat down to his eggs with a not unsuccessful air of *insouciance*. The baby, I suspect, was in the kitchen, cooling down that wonderful complexion, and her mother would doubtless have gone to look for her there, had I not meanwhile entangled her into a complicated discussion anent the manufacture of Kirschwasser, a specialty of this village. Thirty thousand kronen a liter, she vowed, was what they were asking for it. Who was going to pay thirty thousand kronen? Well, it struck me that one shilling and sixpence for a bottle and a quarter of the finest Kirschwasser on earth was a fairly reasonable price.

So far good. I came well out of that little episode....

Endless are the other things we have left undone. Why, we have not even been up the Walserthal, nor so much as an inch in the direction of that fairest of all our alps, the Gamperdona behind Nenzing, where twelve hundred cows are munching and mooing day and night. (The Montavon valley may take care of itself; it is full of tourists). And of hills, real hills, nothing has been climbed save the poor old Scesaplana. I had intended to take Mr. R. on some mountain which has more flavor to it, even though it be not so high—the Drei Schwestern, for instance, above Frastanz, about which my father also wrote a paper; or the Widderstein, or the Kanisfluh. There, on the Kanisfluh, he might have satisfied his craving for edelweiss.

No matter. The mountains can wait for another season.

One is sorry, none the less, not to have witnessed the boisterous procession of cattle returning from their summer pastures, the woodlands changing to gold, and that first September hoar-frost which melts at noon, when drops of moisture glisten on every spider-web; sorry not to have seen the gay fungus-people starting out of the dank earth. And here are plums on their trees, almost ripe. Such a crop there never was. Another week, and they would have been ready to be converted into the first of those ambrosial tarts which are smothered, at the last moment, under a deluge of whipped cream and then devoured so dutifully that, on rising from table, you cannot but feel a kind of bewildered reverence for the capacity of the human stomach. Only another week: how provoking!

No matter. We have had a breath of fresh air together.

THE END